# "Thank you for saving me—both times.

"And for bringing me home and turning on the lights." Cass giggled a little nervously. "I'll probably leave them on all night and think I hear burglars."

"I've got a solution for that." Although the rest of Wade's face showed nothing, his blue eyes were now filled with hot summer fire.

"What?" Cass murmured.

"This." He took a step closer and framed her face with his palms. Then he dropped his head and moved his tongue slowly along her bottom lip.

Cass whimpered and put her hands on his shoulders to hold herself up. He tilted her head back. "Open your mouth, baby. I want a taste of that, too."

Cass's lips dropped open all by themselves. His tongue probed inside, then came out to her bottom lip again. She stood there, clutching him, her head held back by his hands as he thoroughly and methodically nibbled and licked and tasted every part of her mouth.

No other part of his body touched her—just his mouth. It wasn't really a kiss, Cass thought hazily. It was more like an exploration, and my, oh, my, it felt delicious.

Abruptly Wade stepped back to survey her. "That take your mind off burglars?"

"W-what?"

He grinned with smug satisfaction. "Guess it did."

Dear Reader,

By popular demand, Rebels & Rogues returns to Temptation! Over the years we've received lots of positive fan mail about this popular series. You told us how much you love stories that focus on the hero—and wanted more. Well, we've listened. Rebels & Rogues books will appear in the lineup several times a year.

This month's Rebels & Rogues title is written by Alyssa Dean, who made quite a splash with her debut novel, *Mad About You*, published earlier this year. *Romantic Times* said: "Alyssa Dean creates magic in this fantastical excursion into the fun side of romance and sensuality."

Alyssa also brings strong and interesting characters to life. Wade Brillings is the personification of the strong hero and yet he hasn't been bothered much about women. He thinks they're more trouble than they're worth. Of course, he hasn't learned the real meaning of the word trouble—or love—until he saves Cassandra Lloyd's life. And that all happens on the first page of the book!

Look for a new Rebels & Rogues story in September, #556 *The Texan* by Janice Kaiser.

Enjoy!

Birgit Davis-Todd
Senior Editor, Harlequin Temptation

# THE LAST HERO
## Alyssa Dean

## *Harlequin Books*

TORONTO • NEW YORK • LONDON
AMSTERDAM • PARIS • SYDNEY • HAMBURG
STOCKHOLM • ATHENS • TOKYO • MILAN
MADRID • WARSAW • BUDAPEST • AUCKLAND

For Aileen,
My sister and my dearest friend
You're the best, kiddo

ISBN 0-373-25651-5

THE LAST HERO

Copyright © 1995 by Patsy McNish.

**Printed in U.S.A.**

# 1

WHAT WAS that little lady doing here at this hour?

Wade asked himself that question as soon as he saw the fluffy-haired brunette step out of the rapid-transit-station doorway. The woman was just asking for trouble. It was too cold, too dark and too deserted for someone like her to be here all on her lonesome. If she were his little lady, he'd . . .

Where had that thought originated? Wade rubbed one eye, wondering what had come over him. He seldom noticed women anymore, and he rarely imagined himself with one. The cold Calgary air must be doing something to his brain.

It was eleven o'clock at night, and although he'd been told Calgary winters were mild, the temperature was cold enough to freeze important parts off a brass monkey. This rapid-transit parking lot, designed to hold hundreds of cars, was now occupied by only a few dozen chilly-looking vehicles.

Wade had been sitting in one of those vehicles for almost an hour, getting colder and colder with each passing minute. He was tempted to start the engine to get some heat going, but a running car in an almost empty lot would just attract attention. And the man he was supposed to meet had specified that he didn't want attention.

Wade's instructions had been very clear: stay inconspicuous until he was certain the man in the black suede jacket was alone. Then he could show himself.

Wade had chosen a parking space about ten rows from the entrance to the station. It gave him a clear view of the doors and, with the use of his rearview mirrors, a clear view of everything happening in the lot behind him.

Not that much was happening. If the mystery man didn't show soon, Wade was going to leave. Sneaking around parking lots in the middle of the night wasn't his usual way to pass the time, and he felt like a darn fool doing it now. But that phone call had made him curious.

So had the brunette. She paused at the doorway of the station, a cute little figure, about five-five, wearing tan pants and a waist-length brown coat, covered with bright-blue beadwork. The lighting was too dim for Wade to clearly make out her features, but from the way she was glancing around, he guessed she was totally confused.

Small and helpless, he decided. It wasn't anything to do with her being female. Wade knew very few women, and the ones he did know were neither small nor helpless. Actually, he knew more men with those characteristics, all civilians, of course. He didn't dislike them, but at times he wondered how they managed to get through life without a major disaster.

He did a quick check of the place, noting that the passengers who had disembarked with the brunette were already gone. She was still deciding which way to go.

Small, helpless and indecisive, he amended. He turned his head to watch a dark sedan pull into the lot and choose a place beside a gold Camaro two rows in front of him, and almost directly in line with the brunette. She started across the parking lot, carefully picking her way through the slushy snow on heels far too high for such conditions. A man in the sedan climbed out and approached the Camaro.

The brunette let out a yell loud enough for Wade to hear. "Hey!" she shouted. Her cautious steps changed into a run. "What are you doing? That's not your car!"

The fellow beside the Camaro ignored her completely and yanked open the driver's door. As he began to slide inside, the brunette launched herself at the car, landing halfway across the hood in a puff of snowflakes.

Wade stared at the scene in stunned amazement. She might be small, but she was neither helpless nor indecisive. A little too gutsy, maybe, but there wasn't anything wrong with that. "Good for you, baby," he muttered.

She slid to her feet, still shouting, and grabbed the arm of what Wade assumed was a potential car thief. The man gave her an impatient shove, and she shoved back, kicking at him with those deadly heels, shouting for him to leave the car alone.

Wade took a hopeful look around the parking lot. He had a lot of good reasons for remaining inconspicuous, but he didn't want to see the brave little brunette get hurt.

She was going to get more than hurt. Her attacker shoved her to the ground. Then, unbelievably, his hand began a quick flick of movement toward the inside of his jacket, a gesture Wade had seen a hundred times before.

Wade growled an oath and was out of his car and halfway to the Camaro before the man's hand reappeared. Apparently he was the last hero around and the brunette was going to need one. She might have a lot of guts, but he was willing to bet she wasn't prepared to deal with this.

THE MAN WAS HOLDING a gun.

At least, Cassandra presumed it was. She'd never seen a real one before, and she didn't get much of a look at this one. First she was on the hood of the car, then she was on the ground, staring up at a sinister figure with a gun in his hand, a gun he was pointing at her! Her heart gave a huge, horrible, painful jump of terror, while her mind flashed the incredibly ridiculous regret that she wouldn't get a chance to fix the collar on Mrs. Guildcrest's mauve silk jacket.

Then there was a sharp crack. The gun she'd been staring at was in the snow. The gunman was holding his wrist and staring off into the foggy darkness toward the rear of the Camaro.

"How about if you leave the little lady alone," suggested a haunting voice with a hint of an American drawl.

Cass peered in the direction of the voice, but all she could see was dark.

"Stay down, lady!" ordered the drawl. "You there can get—"

He was interrupted by another gunshot, this one coming from the sedan settled beside the Camaro. Cass glanced at it. There was another man, and as she watched he dropped out of sight, behind the sedan.

Cass looked back at her attacker in time to see him turn toward Mark's Camaro. "No, you don't!" she shrieked. She jumped to her feet and made a frantic leap after him.

A huge shape hurtled out of the darkness and tackled her. A gun fired, then another from right above her, making her ears ring. Cass couldn't do anything—she was facedown in a pile of snow, held there by the heavy body sprawled across her back and a hand that kept her head firmly in place.

"Stay put!" growled the voice above her.

Definitely an American, Cass decided. He sounded like those tourist people who came into her store during Stampede week.

As for the staying-put part, Cass didn't have much choice with a big male body on top of her, pressing her into the cold ground. She lay there, stunned, panting, listening. It sounded as if the thieves were leaving. There was the noise of car doors slamming, followed by the sound of tires spinning across frozen snow, then silence.

"They're gone," the American informed her. "Goddamn it, lady, you're lucky to get out of that alive!"

Cass lifted her head one inch, and it was immediately shoved back down. "Thank you," she gurgled. "Let me up. I . . ."

He shifted his weight off her, but kept one knee on her back and one hand on her head. "That Camaro yours?"

"It belongs to my cousin," Cass panted. "Can you get off me? Please!"

"Almost got yourself killed over it!" He bent lower, so his breath touched her ear. "You did fine, honey. But next time you're caught in crossfire, keep your goddamn head down!"

Before Cass could explain that she didn't ever plan on being in another gun battle, the pressure holding her down was gone. She raised her head and looked around.

The cold, silent shape of the Camaro was on her left. The car thieves were nowhere in sight, and neither was anyone else. There was no sound, no noise, nothing to suggest any other human being was out here.

Cass climbed numbly to her feet, wondering if she had imagined the whole thing, and bent to dust the snow off her clothes. Her head jerked up as a car started not far away. She bent her head to avoid the glare of its headlights, and as the car drove away, she saw an object lying in the snow, right beside Mark's Camaro. She removed her glove to pick it up.

It was a round, silver medallion, on a long, broken chain.

"YOU'RE SURE you're all right?" Lydia asked for the third time.

"I'm fine," Cass insisted. She sipped at her coffee and sighed as she watched her business partner pace back and forth across the white-tiled floor of the combination sewing room-office at the back of their boutique. She shouldn't have mentioned last night's little adventure to Lydia. She hadn't intended to get into a long discussion about it, but this morning she had been just aching to confide in someone. Now she was sorry.

Lydia made another pass of the room, a narrow figure sheathed in a vivid shade of red. Her jet-black hair swirled as she turned, and Cass absently noted that not one single strand showed any gray. Lydia might be well over fifty, but her hair certainly wasn't going to give her away.

She stopped in front of Cass and pushed her hands deep into her pockets. "You should have reported this to the police last night."

"Why?" asked Cass. She shifted in the chair beside her white sewing desk and sipped at her coffee. "What would they do?"

"What would they do?" Lydia made an exasperated gesture with her hand. "They'd find those car thieves.

They'd speak with that man who rescued you. They'd—"

"They couldn't do that," Cass interrupted. "I can't tell them what anybody looked like. I saw the gun briefly. I could describe it. I could probably even draw a picture of it, but I don't think the police could catch somebody from that. Do you?"

"No, but—"

"And that man who helped me mustn't have wanted to talk to the police." Cass felt rather triumphant about discerning this. "Otherwise he wouldn't have left."

"He might have been a criminal, as well! You—"

"I don't think so." Cass recalled the drawling voice, the large, shadowy figure, the feeling of his body landing on hers, protecting her. "I think he was a nice person who didn't want to have to answer a lot of questions. Neither did I. Besides, the police would just laugh at me."

"Laugh at you? Darling, I don't think—"

"They would so, Lydia! Remember what happened a couple of months ago when that weird guy shoplifted a bunch of our stuff? Every time I spoke, that big policeman in the dismal gray coat started laughing."

Lydia drew in a long breath and looked as if she were going to laugh, too. "That was because you were describing the undergarments the man took. You did rather go on and on about how they would look on him, and—" her shoulders shook slightly "—and the colors he should have stolen."

"Well really, why would a man like that steal a white camisole? He would obviously look better in red! Or even that lovely smoky orange we—"

"Yes, dear," Lydia interrupted. "But this is entirely different."

"No, it isn't." Cass picked up her cup. "There was no point in talking to the police. I couldn't tell them anything. They'd think I was funny, and besides, it was late. I just wanted to go home."

Lydia tapped a perfectly manicured fingernail against her bottom lip. "Why were you there so late?"

"Picking up Mark's car. He asked me to get it for him."

"Why couldn't he get himself?"

"He was on his way out of town," Cass explained. "He said he didn't have time to go home, and he wanted me to pick up his car and take care of his hamster. The last time I borrowed his car I forget to return the keys, so it was no problem." She smiled slightly as she thought about Mark. Her cousin did so many favors for her it was nice to be able to return one.

"He had no business asking you to go there at that time of night," Lydia pronounced. "He should have—"

"He didn't know it was going to be late. He called just past six." Cass frowned into her coffee. "I was going to ask Charlie to take me, but after our argument . . ."

"Argument!" Lydia exclaimed. "*You* had an argument with somebody?"

"It wasn't exactly an argument," Cass mumbled. She bent her head. "Charlie thinks I should be saving up to buy a car of my own."

"I thought you were."

"I was, but I stopped." Cass stretched out her legs and examined her shoes. "Do you like these?"

Lydia glanced down at them and frowned. "Italian?"

"Yes. Aren't they lovely?"

"Gorgeous. Three hundred dollars?"

"Three-fifty." Cass admired them again. "They're worth it, too, even if Charlie didn't think so."

Lydia's gaze moved from the shoes to Cass's face. "You broke up over a pair of shoes?"

"It wasn't just the shoes."

"Oh?"

"It's everything about me." Cass looked ruefully over at her more-than-competent business partner. "I'm not the sort of woman men like."

"You're not the sort of woman men like?" Lydia repeated. She laughed incredulously. "Good heavens, Cass, your social life would make a movie star jealous."

"Oh, they like me fine until they get to know me." Cass picked up a blue-handled seam ripper and turned it in her fingers. "I am not good wife material. Men these days want a woman who can manage a career, a family, a husband and a house while the men spend fourteen hours a day talking on their cellular phones to one another."

Lydia put a consoling hand on Cass's shoulder. "I don't think that's really the case."

"Yes, it is. Look at you and Tom. You take care of everything, including this store. Tom just runs around being an oil executive."

"He has other uses," Lydia murmured. "Besides, I've been married for ages. I'm sure you'd—"

"No, I wouldn't." Cass pouted unseeing at the desk in front of her. "Face it, Lydia, the practicalities of reality are beyond me."

"The practicalities of reality? Who said that? Charlie?"

"Yes. And he's right. They are."

Lydia leaned against the sewing table. "Is that why Charlie broke it off with you?"

"Oh, Charlie didn't break it off with me. He was perfectly willing to fix me." Cass blinked up into Lydia's concerned face. "The thing is, I don't think I'm fixable. I'm trying, but the best I can hope for is slightly above awful."

Lydia patted her shoulder. "There's nothing wrong with you, honey."

"There's plenty wrong with me. I am twenty-nine years old and I can hardly take care of myself, let alone a family."

"That's not really—"

"Yes, it is," Cass insisted. "Just look at my life. I grew up on a farm, and I don't know anything about farming. My brothers did everything. I was supposed to learn how to take care of a house, and I never did. Finally, my mother just gave up and did it herself."

"That was years ago, honey. You—"

"That was last summer! I went back home to help Mom when she had her operation, and I was utterly useless. My sisters-in-law already had everything under control. All I did was make new clothes for everybody!"

"They were probably gorgeous," Lydia soothed.

"They were," Cass agreed. "But that wasn't what I went there to do." She motioned around the store. "And look at this place. You had this store before you hired me right out of design school. I just make the clothes. I'm hopeless at doing even basic stuff like taking the cash. And I don't have one clue about ordering stock."

"You do all the designing and all the sewing," Lydia reminded her. "You're very good at it. Everyone says so."

"Do they?" Cass's mood brightened a little, only to darken almost immediately. "The rest of my life is just as bad. I live in a house I rent from one of *your* relatives, and you found it for me. I don't own a car, because whenever I need one, I use Mark's. When anything goes wrong, I have to get someone to fix it for me. I don't do anything for anybody, and everyone does everything for me."

"That's absolutely untrue!" Lydia exclaimed. "You're a very warmhearted person, darling. And you do things for Mark. Why, last night, you picked up his car for him."

"I almost forgot about that car," Cass confessed. "After the argument with Charlie, it had completely slipped my mind. Then I remembered about Herman...."

"Herman?"

"Mark's hamster, the one I gave him for his birthday. I remembered him and the car, and I had to take a bus and then the train to get it. After the incident in the parking lot, I just went home." She gave Lydia an anxious look. "Herman would be okay on his own for one night, wouldn't he?"

Lydia's lips twitched slightly. "I'm sure he's fine. But . . ."

"Mark's lucky," Cass mused. "You probably haven't noticed, but at times he isn't real good at the practicalities of reality, either. But he's a man. Sooner or later he'll find a woman who's good at taking care of things and she'll take care of him. As for me, I am not good wife material."

Lydia examined her fingertips. "Did Charlie say that?"

"No. He thought I had potential, but when he starting talking about it, I realized it was a conversation I've had a zillion times before. I have so many 'too' somethings wrong with me that trying to change them all is impossible."

"Cass . . ."

"It's true," Cass insisted. "And I am really tired of hearing about it. I am not dating anyone who is interested in finding a wife ever again. It's a waste of their time. Every man I meet can do everything better than I can. They don't need me for anything."

Lydia squeezed her shoulder. "You just haven't found the right man, honey."

"I'm not sure the right man exists," Cass replied. "The only one I've met who would be perfect is Mark. He and I get along just fine. He never finds anything wrong with me, because he has all the same faults I do." She sighed with resignation. "Unless I find one, you and Mark, and Mark's future wife, will be stuck taking care of me for the rest of my life."

"I don't mind a bit." Lydia returned to her desk. "I do think you're wrong, though. There isn't one thing the matter with you, Cass, and I'd like to wring Charlie's neck for making you feel so bad."

"You don't have to do that." Cass forced a smile. "I'm pretending he doesn't exist." She gave Charlie a few last seconds of thought. She hadn't been all that wild about him, but his comments had depressed her.

She glanced at the mauve suit jacket hanging on the dress form in the corner of the room and felt instantly better. Lydia was right—she did make wonderful clothes. Except for the collar, that suit was marvelous. "I should be able to finish Marion Guildcrest's suit today if I can get the collar . . ."

Lydia gave a little dismayed gasp. "Oh, I almost forgot! Sue Hammond phoned me at home this morning. Do you remember her? She's my second cousin's husband's niece-in-law—from his first marriage, of course."

"Oh?" Cass hadn't been able to follow the blood-lines, but that wasn't anything unusual. Lydia Temple seemed to be related to over sixty percent of Calgary. She closed her eyes and thought about it. "I remember her. Lovely auburn hair. Last time she wanted a dress that matched her dishes. I had place settings spread all over the store."

"That's her, but this time she wants something that goes with her drapes. You'll have to go over to her house to see them. I said you'd stop by after lunch. You can, can't you? She lives in Lakeview, south of the military base. I'll write out directions."

"Of course I can." Their little boutique, Creative Elegance, was successful because of Lydia's business sense, the large number of her friends and relations, along with Cass's talent for dressmaking and material selection. A personalized consultation might take a lot of time, but it also kept the customers coming in. "Did Sue mention any colors?"

"Green and gold." Lydia turned toward the sample cupboard. "I'll sort out what I think will suit her. You'd better take bolts, not samples. Sue will want to toss them all over the place."

"Put in that new aqua and gray that just arrived," Cass suggested. She removed the suit jacket from the dress form and carried it back to the sewing table.

Lydia stopped at the doorway. "I do wish you'd talk to the police about last night."

"I can't tell them anything," Cass murmured. "I didn't get a good look at anybody."

"What about the fellow who rescued you? I know it was nice of him, but we can't have armed vigilantes driving around Calgary, no matter how good their intentions. Maybe you—"

"I'm certainly not going to turn him in to the police!" Cass exclaimed. "He probably saved my life. Besides, I . . . I can't identify him, either."

"Really?" Lydia sounded a bit skeptical. "You're sure? You're not holding back to protect him, are you?"

"Of course not." Cass began unpicking the collar seam.

"You're sure?"

"I didn't see him, Lydia. I really didn't."

Lydia hovered in the doorway a moment, then turned. Cass waited until the tap of Lydia's heels indicated the older woman was out of the room, then took a quick over-the-shoulder look to make sure. Lydia's reference to the military base had given her an idea. She drew the silver medallion from her purse, closed her fingers around it and shut her eyes.

The heat started from her fingertips and wound its way up her arm. An image floated in front of her closed eyes: a big man, with a blunt-nosed face, summer-sky eyes and sandy-red hair trimmed close to his scalp. His lips were full and sensuous, although the rest of his appearance was that of tough concentration.

Before the image faded, she got a brief impression of a navy blue uniform and the flash of medals.

# 2

THIS WAS a very practical thing to do, Cass decided as she stopped her car in front of the barricade to the military base. She was certain the medallion belonged to her rescuer, and she knew for a fact it had been in his family for some time. He shouldn't lose it because he'd done a good deed.

She rolled down her window so she could speak to the young, blank-faced guard inside the white booth. "I wonder if you can help me. I'm looking for someone."

The man lifted an eyebrow.

"He's a big man with sandy-red hair and...uh...an American accent," Cass went on. "Sort of a...drawl?"

The guard stared at her. "Name?"

"I don't know." Cass batted her eyelashes and watched the man's cheeks flush just slightly. "Actually, I don't even know if he's here at all." She went on with her fabrication. "I saw this man drop something, and I'm just...guessing that he might be in the military."

The guard frowned and said nothing.

"He sort of looked like he might be," Cass continued. "I thought I'd just check here, in case he...uh...is." She pulled the medallion out of her pocket and held it up. "This kind of looks military, and..."

The guard shoved a hand out of the sliding-glass window, took the medallion and examined it. "It looks like it's from the Civil War era, ma'am."

"That's what I thought," Cass agreed. "If you have any Americans staying here, you could check . . ." She stopped talking because the guard wasn't listening. He'd picked up a phone receiver in his booth and was speaking into it. Cass shifted uneasily in her seat.

Finally the guard hung up. "All right." He nodded. "You give me your name and address. If this doesn't belong to anyone here, we'll have it returned to you."

"Thank you." Cass handed over a business card. "I'm sure he'll be glad to get it back."

She turned carefully in the narrow circle and aimed the car toward Sue Hammond's house, feeling immensely pleased with herself. There. She'd done the right thing, although it was too bad she wouldn't get to meet that man. There had been something rather hypnotic about his image. She tried to conjure it up again, but without the medallion in her hand, it was difficult to remember.

As she turned the car into Mrs. Hammond's driveway she wondered if the guard had really believed her story. It did sound rather ridiculous, but the truth would sound a lot stranger.

Actually, she'd never told anybody about her ability to "read" images off inanimate objects. When she was studying dress design at the local college, she'd discovered that if she held a swatch of material in her hand and concentrated, she could picture what it would look like on a person. Quite by accident, she'd tried the same concentration technique with a watch she'd found, and to her surprise, she'd received a hazy image of the owner. It was a fitful talent—sometimes it worked and sometimes it didn't—but if she did receive an image, it was always correct.

It was in this case, too. Cass was positive of that. He might not be in the military, but she had received the impression of a uniform. And somebody with military training certainly fitted the man who'd come to her rescue.

Maybe he'd be incredibly grateful. He would have her name from her card. He just might search her out to thank her. No, he probably wouldn't do that. He might think she would tell the police who he was. Then again, that image didn't look like someone who'd be the least bit concerned about police.

"SO WHEN THIS character didn't show, you amused yourself by using one of our parking lots for target practice, eh?" Evan McCleod scowled around his barren little office, then over at Wade. "Why can't you foreigners save that stuff for your own country? You must have parking lots down there."

"We're requisitioning some," Wade grunted. He'd been ordered to turn this mess over to the Royal Canadian Mounted Police. No one had said he'd enjoy doing it, and he wasn't.

He'd also been told to deal with RCMP Inspector Evan McCleod, and Wade wasn't enjoying that, either. McCleod wasn't a bad sort, but he had his own views of how Wade should have handled the situation. As Wade watched the burly, middle-aged man glower at him, he wished McCleod would consider keeping those views to himself.

"Make sure they come with brunettes!" Evan suggested. "What did you say—about five-five?"

"Yup. Five-five, one hundred and twenty pounds, late twenties." Wade could have added a lot of other information, like the sway of her hips when she walked, the smell of her hair and the way her body had felt squirming under his. He didn't understand why he remembered all those things, or why he was thinking about them now.

He pushed her to the back of his mind, where she'd been hovering since last night, and focused on Evan. "You sure she didn't report it?"

"Positive." Evan's heavy-eyed face radiated disapproval. "I get a summary from the Calgary police every morning. I'd remember reading about something like that."

Wade tugged on his bottom lip. He had been positive the little lady would be hollering for the police the moment he left. But she hadn't. If she were a man, he'd think she was trying to hide something. A woman... Well, he wasn't sure. Maybe Evan knew. "Why wouldn't she?"

"Who knows?" Evan grumbled. "Maybe she was scared you'd come back."

That sounded pretty ridiculous. "Why in hell would she be scared of me?"

One of Evan's brown eyebrows arched. "Good Lord, man, I'd be scared of you under those circumstances. And a woman..." His voice trailed off as if it were obvious.

"Yeah?" Wade encouraged. "What about a woman?"

"She'd probably be terrified!" A frown furrowed Evan's wide forehead. "Are you not married, Commander?"

Wade shook his head. Marriage was something he'd never even considered.

"Ever been?"

"Nope."

"Huh!" Evan's gray eyes were suddenly a lot sharper. "Don't tell me there's something you aren't an expert about?"

"How's that?"

"You're one of the navy's special services men. You were described as an expert in armed combat, unarmed combat, covert surveillance... The list went on and on."

Wade didn't consider his accomplishments anything to brag about. It was just the way things were. "I've been around awhile."

"You can't be more than forty," Evan scoffed.

"Thirty-nine," Wade corrected. "Been with the navy since I was eighteen. That's a good number of years."

"And somehow you missed the finer points of dealing with women, eh?"

Wade felt slightly embarrassed about his lack of knowledge. "Not a whole lot of women in my line of work."

"What about this 'woman in every port' rumor? Don't—"

"Never found 'em worth the trouble," Wade grunted. His thoughts returned to the little lady. "You really figure she took off because I scared her?"

"I'm just guessing." Evan seemed a trifle amused. "Women aren't as predictable as, say, an M-16 rifle."

Wade vaguely remembered hearing other men complain of the same thing, although he'd never paid much attention. "That so?"

"Yeah, that's so." Evan studied him for a long moment "She could have other reasons for not calling the police. Maybe she didn't want the publicity, either."

Wade didn't say anything.

"That's why you took off, isn't it? If the city police had gotten you, the press would have splashed your picture all over North America—U.S. Military In Shoot-out At The O.K. Rapid Transit." Evan looked as if the prospect pleased him. "Don't suppose the folks back home would like that, would they?"

Wade had no problem imagining General Durant's reaction, which was why he'd retreated and why he'd made certain the brunette couldn't identify him. However, he wasn't trying to avoid the consequences, just the publicity. "You want me to go talk to the city boys?"

"Not unless you can identify those car thieves. Can you?"

"Nope." Wade was sorry he couldn't. One of those men had shot at him and he wanted the chance to politely take him aside and tell him not to do it again.

"And you can't do a composite of the brunette?"

"Nope," Wade repeated. He wished he'd paid closer attention to the brunette's features. He wouldn't mind tracking her down, either, to ask her why she hadn't reported the incident, and he'd chew her out but good for being there in the first place.

"Then there's no point in your seeing the Calgary police," Evan pronounced. "You don't seem to have much information and we don't need any press on this. It might put that fellow you were supposed to meet in a lot of trouble." He shot Wade a hard look. "He didn't give you any indication of who he was when he phoned you?"

Wade shook his head. "He said he worked for Orion, thought a meeting might be in both our best interests and invited me to pick him up at the Brentwood rapid-transit station. Never gave me a name or even a description. Just told me he'd be wearing a black suede jacket. That's how I was supposed to recognize him."

"Orion, eh?" Evan shuffled a few papers around on his desk. "The weapons dealer?"

"That's right." Wade scowled as he considered the headaches Orion's bunch had caused him. "Supposed to be an American, although no one knows his true identity. He's got a real nice little operation going. Steals experimental weapons from whoever has 'em and sells them to whoever wants 'em."

Evan glanced at a page, then back up. "You've had dealings with Orion before, I understand."

Wade hesitated, then nodded. He knew the RCMP had been told most of the details by his own superiors. "A few years back Orion's men hit one of our naval research stations. Took something we didn't want him to have. Navy sent in a team of us to get it back."

"And you did?"

"Uh-huh." Wade had never felt very pleased with those results. It had been a fairly successful operation, but they hadn't captured Orion himself. "We tracked down a couple of the small fry, and got enough information to intercept when the item was being turned over to the buyer." The whole thing came back to him— the dark night, the cabin cruiser moored off the coast of an unfriendly country... They would have had Orion then if the man hadn't blown up his own boat, along with his own men and the buyer, just so he could get away. Wade's team had been darn lucky to get out of there without significant collateral damage and casualties.

He pushed the memories into the past where they belonged. "We didn't get Orion, but we put a real cramp in his style. He lost his top men and spooked potential buyers. He hasn't been much of a problem in the States since. Rumor has it he slunk off to South America, but he could have decided to come up to Canada and rebuild his operation from here."

"We don't want him," Evan said fervently. "I hear he's not a real nice person to have around."

"He's damned unpleasant," Wade grunted. Naval Intelligence had tried a couple of times to infiltrate the group, and what had happened to their agents hadn't been pleasant at all. "I'd like to get my hands on him."

"I'm sure you would." Evan's expression became stern. "Still, you should have called us before . . ."

Wade was getting mighty tired of hearing what he should have done. "I didn't have time to do that," he snapped. "That fellow took one hell of a chance contacting me. Orion wouldn't treat a double cross real kindly."

"I understand that, but we—"

"He wanted me there right away. By the time I traipsed through all your red tape, it would have been next Thursday."

"That's not how we—"

"As for the woman, I wasn't about to sit in my car and watch her take a bullet, either!"

Evan wasn't backing down. "You had no business being there armed! We don't go in for that sort of crap up here."

"That so?" Wade snarled. "Criminals get weapons, but the military don't?"

Evan glowered at him for a long moment, then slowly chuckled. "I guess you've got a point there." He tapped his fingers on the desk. "Look, I'll talk to the city police and smooth things over for you. How's that?"

Wade could recognize an olive branch when he saw one. "Appreciate it."

"This fellow in the black suede jacket might have been spooked by all that commotion. He could contact you again."

"He could," Wade agreed. "Or he could be history—if Orion figured out what he had planned."

"Another possibility," Evan agreed glumly. "If we find anything suspicious, I'll let you know. In the meantime, I don't want you conducting your own investigation. If you hear from this black-suede-jacket character again, I want to know about it. Before any meeting happens."

Wade considered it for moment and nodded.

"And in the meantime, Commander Brillings, stay out of dark parking lots and away from brunettes."

"I'M BACK," Cass called out as she set the box on the back counter.

Lydia tapped into the room. "Oh, there you are. I was just closing up. Did Susan make up her mind?"

"Finally." Cass hung up her coat. "It was a toss-up between the gold and the aqua. The aqua looked best on Susan, but the gold looks best with her drapes." She threw up her hands. "I wish I hadn't shown her that mustard print shantung. It took me ages to talk her out of it."

"What's wrong with the mustard print?" Lydia asked.

"Nothing. It's Susan!" Cass thought of the blond, rather rotund woman she'd just left. "She'd look like an underdone, overrelished sausage in it."

Lydia pressed a palm against her forehead. "I hope you didn't use those exact words when you were talking to her."

"Of course not," Cass assured her. "I was very tactful. Were you busy this afternoon?"

"No. The cold weather is keeping all the customers away. I unpacked stock. We've got the nicest line of scarves in, but I'm not happy with that new jewelry I ordered. You'll have to take a look at it tomorrow and see what you think." Lydia chose her own knee-length black wool coat from the rack. "It's past five, Cass. You aren't staying, are you?"

Cass was already opening the portfolio she'd taken with her. "I'm just going to finish designing Mrs. Hammond's dress. Then I'll go over to Mark's and pick up Herman."

Lydia buttoned her coat. "You, uh, didn't change your mind about calling the police?"

"Who?" Cass glanced at the sketches she'd made. "Oh, them. No. I'm just going to forget about it." Unless, of course, the hunky medallion owner stopped by to thank her. "Good night, Lydia. I'll try and be on time tomorrow."

Lydia hovered at the door for a moment, then sighed a concerned good-night and left.

Cass locked the door behind her and began unpacking the box of material she'd brought in with her. She usually enjoyed the silence, but as the store settled into its usual nighttime quiet, she began to feel edgy. Perhaps that was because of what had happened last night.

She wandered cautiously into the front of the store and checked the door. The display cases containing silky scarves and frivolous underwear mocked her discomfort. The few items of jewelry were locked in the safe, along with the small amount of cash they kept on hand. The alarm was set. She was perfectly, perfectly safe here.

She returned to the sewing room, pulled out the last item from the box. She'd found it in Mark's car—thrown on the floor in the back. It was a rather worn black suede jacket with a ripped pocket. Cass had brought it inside to mend the rip.

She held up the jacket to examine the damage and shivered. The black material felt very cold and unpleasant and increased her feeling of unease. She decided to mend it right away and then forget about it. As she examined the tear, she wondered about the square gray box thing she'd also found on the back floor of the car. She'd assumed it was a hamster toy of some sort that had tumbled out of the bag on the seat. It could have come from this pocket, though. The rip was certainly large enough.

The object didn't seem particularly important. She would put it in Herman's cage, and if he didn't know what to do with it, she'd take it out. She finished repairing the pocket and hung the jacket beside her coat, so she'd remember to take it with her when she went to Mark's place.

Then she began modifying the pattern for Mrs. Hammond's new dress. The task absorbed all her attention. The aqua and gray would have been better, but the gold was going to look all right, especially in the drop-waisted, wide-skirted effect she was going to design. The store was silent except for the crinkling of the tissue paper.

"Cassandra Lloyd?" asked a deep male voice.

Cass dropped her pencil and whirled around.

A large figure stood in the doorway leading to the back hall. "We're closed," Cass announced around a swallow.

The man ignored that and took a step out of the shadows into the room. Cass blinked and her breath stopped entirely.

First there was the scent—hot and steamy—not after-shave, just plain male. Then there was the size of him—a man so big that the room seemed to contract when he stepped into it. He folded his arms across his chest, his legs spread shoulder-width apart, his summer-blue eyes narrow and almost wary. Cass felt a huge surge of triumph. That shadowy image from the medallion had been dead-on, and was standing right here in her store. "Oh, my," she said.

He appraised her without changing his expression. "You Cassandra Lloyd?"

"That's right." He wasn't wearing his uniform. Instead, he had on blue jeans, a thigh-length, sheepskin-lined denim jacket and brown boots that passed his calves. The jeans—Wranglers, she decided—looked about two years old. No, more like three—the way that stitching down the seams . . .

"I'm Wade Brillings." He took one slow step toward her. "Understand you're looking for me."

"Looking for you?" Cass repeated. His slight drawl and western garb gave the impression of a cowboy, not a military man. He was here, though, so he must have received his medallion and her business card. She must have been right about the military connection, too.

She continued to study him. What would he be wearing under that jacket? A brown cable-knit sweater, maybe? And probably a T-shirt under that. Let's see...khaki colored? She moved her gaze up his square jaw, and stopped when she reached the grim, straight line that was his mouth. "I'm not really...that is I...uh..."

He stared at her in cold, dead silence. "Well? You got a message for me?"

"A message?" Cass shook her head. "Uh...no. But, um...I did want to thank you for what you did and...um..."

His forehead creased with furrows. "What in hell are you talking about?"

"The parking lot," Cass reminded him. "Last night. You—"

He waved a hand to silence her and yanked the silver medallion out of his jacket pocket. "You dropped this off at the guardhouse today?"

"Oh, you got it!" Cass gave him a big smile. "That's wonderful." Her smile faltered as she realized he wasn't smiling back. "You don't have to worry," she assured him. "I didn't tell the police, so . . ."

The mouth didn't change. "What is it you didn't tell the police?"

"That it was you. You're probably not supposed to shoot people." She realized that sounded dumb. "I mean, of course you can shoot people. You're in the military. But you can't shoot just anybody, can you?"

Apart from one eyebrow lifting slightly, not a single muscle on the man moved. "Let's start over, Miss Lloyd. Where did you get this medallion?"

"In the parking lot. You must have dropped—"

"What parking lot was this?"

"The Brentwood rapid-transit parking lot." Boy, this guy had thighs. Not fat, but not lean, either. Heavy. Muscled. Cass sucked in her lower lip and tried to concentrate on the conversation. "You must remember," she encouraged. "Last night. Some men were stealing my cousin's car. You shot at them. You—"

His voice whipped out to interrupt her. "You say you saw me shooting up some parking lot last night?"

A slow, freezing shiver crept up Cass's spine. His face was awfully cold and awfully blank. He was not happy about this. Suddenly his big shape seemed more sinister than attractive. "I didn't get a good look," she said through a now-dry mouth. "But ... um ... I recognize your voice."

"Ah." The brows lowered. "This sounds like a real fascinating story, Miss Lloyd." He strolled over to rest his bottom against the edge of Lydia's desk. "How about if you tell me the whole thing?"

"You know the whole ..."

He flicked open the buttons on his jacket. "Let's assume I don't. Fill me in."

It wasn't a brown cable-knit sweater—it was dark green, with a high neck that prevented her from seeing any of his chest. However, it looked as massive as the rest of him. Probably covered with that reddish sandy hair. Cass took one long breath and launched into the story.

"And then the thieves drove off," she concluded. "I found that medallion in the snow near Mark's car and—"

"You saw someone drop it there?"

"No, no. I just found it." She watched him straighten, muscle by muscle, and began to wish she had left the medallion alone.

"Look, Miss Lloyd, this isn't making much sense. If you didn't see this character, and you didn't see him drop this medallion, what in hell made you decide it was from a military base?"

It was cold in the shop now, as cold as the icy blue slits of eyes and the scowl on his lips. Cass shivered. "I had the medallion and . . ."

He took a long stride toward her and dangled the medallion in her face. "You saying you got my description and CW—current whereabouts—from this?"

"Yes, I did." She skiddled back as his expression darkened. Those blank, dangerous eyes weren't going to believe she'd done just that. "I mean . . . uh . . . no. I . . . um . . . saw you in the parking lot and . . . um . . ."

"You said you didn't get a good look at the man in the parking lot."

"Yes. I mean, no, I didn't, but . . ."

He swung the medallion in front of her eyes. "There anything on this to suggest who owns it?"

Cass's eyes moved back and forth with the medallion. "N-no, but . . ."

He snapped the dangling medallion into his palm. "Then what in *hell* made you take it directly to the base?"

"I . . . uh . . ." Cass watched his strong fingers curl around the medallion and touched a hand to her slightly dizzy head. "I just thought . . . um . . . the voice was an American and . . . uh . . . there was a gun and . . . the medallion looks kind of military so . . ." She took a breath. "It does belong to you, doesn't it?"

"Uh-huh."

He studied her up and down in total silence, a silence that grew and grew until it was almost another presence in the room. Cass was more than a little scared now. She swallowed a couple of times and tried to think of something to say, but her mind was completely empty.

Finally, he broke the silence. "You tell the police about this?"

"No, I—"

"Why not?"

"Because . . . um . . . because I didn't."

Again he was silent. Then, "You didn't find this medallion in that parking lot. Someone gave it to you. Who was it?"

"No one..."

"This Mark you mentioned. Who is he?"

"Mark? Mark Dowling. He's my cousin."

"He give it to you?"

"No, he..."

Wade closed the distance between them and loomed over her, so close that they were almost touching. "Look, lady, someone gave this to you and told you to have it sent to me. I want a name, and I'm not leaving here without it."

Cass was so terrified now that she'd say anything to make him go. Her cousin was out of town. This thug couldn't do anything to him. "All right," she whispered. "All right...uh...sure, M-Mark gave it to me."

"That's better. What else did he say?"

This was just getting worse and worse. "Uh...he said I should send it to you."

"Why?"

"Because he couldn't himself," Cass gasped. "He...uh...had to leave town."

"Why?"

"I don't know." Cass sucked in some air and then some more. "He just did."

Wade stepped back and glowered at her. "So you thought you'd try a little touch of blackmail. Is that it?"

"Blackmail?" Cass shook her head. "I wouldn't..."

"Oh yes, you would!" He jabbed a finger into her chest. "I don't know what happened last night, but if you think you can use an old medal to blackmail someone in the military, you...are...dead...wrong!" He punctuated the last few words by stabs to her chest.

Cass cupped her teeth over her shaking lower lip and slid back. "I'm not," she insisted. "I don't do... I don't... I'm not trying to blackmail anybody."

There was enough menace on his face to scare ninety-eight percent of Calgary. "You know what we do to blackmailers?"

Cass shook her head, while visions of firing squads and blindfolds leaped into her mind. She shrank from him and an almost imperceptible flicker of satisfaction crossed his face. Cass felt an unfamiliar blur of anger. He was enjoying scaring her. She pushed back her shoulders. "Look, Mr. Wade Brillings, I don't blackmail people. I was just trying to return that medallion. That's all."

"That so? I don't quite see it that way."

Cass wasn't sure if she was going to throw up or pass out. "I don't care how you see it," she gasped. "You have your medallion back, so there really is no reason for you to be here. I want you to leave my store. Now. Or... Or I will call the police!"

For one second, he actually appeared startled. "That supposed to be a threat?"

"Yes!" Cass decided. "Yes, it is."

"Figured as much." He moved toward her again and crowded her back until her legs bumped against the sewing table. His right hand grabbed her chin and held her head up, forcing her to look straight into his nasty, cold eyes. "Don't threaten me, baby," he warned. "And don't try your little scam on me again, either. I don't have to call the police for help." He flicked his hand off her chin and turned toward the door. He stopped by the rack of coats near the doorway and thrust a thumb in the direction of the black suede jacket. "This yours?"

"No . . . uh . . . it's just been repaired."

"Uh-huh." He stared at it for an instant, and then he was gone.

# 3

SHE HAD camouflage eyes.

Wade switched on the car engine and drummed his fingers against the steering wheel. Camouflage eyes. Mottled green and brown like he'd never seen before. He'd been hypnotized by them as soon as he'd walked into that room, by the color and the beckoning admiration in them.

Of course when he'd left that room, those remarkable eyes had been filled with tremendous disappointment.

Damn it all to hell, did she have to look at him like that?

He stroked a thumb across the face of the medallion. He'd known he'd lost this sometime last night, and had resigned himself to never getting it back. When it had shown up on the base, along with a business card, he still hadn't connected "Cassandra Lloyd" with the fluffy-haired brunette.

He'd recognized her immediately, although her clothes were different. Today she had on one of those skirt-looking things, more like shorts, actually, made out of some clingy deep-blue material that swirled around when she moved. She wasn't all that tall, even with those high heels, yet she gave the impression of being composed entirely of legs, an impression he was certain she dressed to achieve.

She'd been nervous, so nervous she'd sucked on her bottom lip, sliding it in and out of her mouth. Every time she'd done it, he'd wondered how it tasted. And those eyes! He gave his head a hard shake, but the memory remained. Camouflage eyes, looking at him as if a bedroom were only a step away. Camouflage eyes, looking at him as if he'd just shot her best friend.

He shoved the medallion back in his pocket. What in hell was the matter with him? That little lady had been on his mind ever since the first time he'd seen her. It was unusual for him to even notice a woman, much less think about her.

Not that he didn't like women. In his youth he'd played around some, not as much as lots of other men did, but enough to get it out of his system. That was years ago. Nowadays, he slept with the odd one, and he worked with a few, but on the whole, he didn't have a lot to do with them.

And this recent conversation with Cass Lloyd proved he was no hell at dealing with them. A man, well, you give a man a thump on the jaw, and he'll likely cough up what he knows. You can't treat a woman like that, certainly not a woman like her.

Scaring her had probably been poor strategy. From the way she'd eyed him, it was obvious she was interested. Maybe he'd have done better if he'd used that. He might have gotten a little more information.

It was too late now. She was scared of him, and she wasn't about to tell him spit. Still, the visit to the shop wasn't a total loss. There was only one person who knew Wade had been in that parking lot, and that was the man he was supposed to have met. Orion's man. The man in the black suede jacket. That man must have given Wade's medallion to Miss Lloyd and asked her to pass it on. Wade wasn't clear why.

He took a look at the city map and eased the car out into the traffic. Time for him to have a little chat with Mr. Mark Dowling.

CASS'S HANDS were still shaking as she parked the car in front of Mark's house. It was that terrible man, she decided. That terrible man and his terrible accusations. Forget it, she told herself. He's a creep, that's all. It was too bad, though—there was something about his great strength that really, really appealed to her. Lousy taste in clothes, though. She closed her eyes and pictured him, redrawing his figure with a loose-fitting white silk shirt, then ripping that off and going for plain, straight cotton. A man like that wouldn't wear silk. Ever.

Mark's narrow bungalow looked dark and somewhat sinister, and the well-treed front lawn hinted at dangerous shapes. You have too much imagination, Cass told herself, but after last night and then tonight, who could blame her? She glanced around anxiously a few times, but there were only a couple of frozen-looking cars on the street, and not a single person anywhere.

The sensation of unease returned when she pushed opened Mark's front door and switched on the hall light. She tried to shake it off as she hung up the black suede jacket she'd brought in with her. Even it appeared sinister tonight. She touched it, absently wondering if it did indeed belong to her cousin. An image floated into her mind of a black-haired stranger with heavy, bushy eyebrows.

Cass dropped her hand and backed away. She really wished she hadn't done that. The man seemed innocent enough, but his image had been accompanied by the same feeling she'd had when she'd mended the jacket, a cold, dull sensation that made her skin crawl. She took a breath, shook it off and wandered into the living room.

The first thing she noticed was that the hamster cage was on the floor; its door was wide open, and Herman was nowhere in sight.

The second thing she noticed was the mess in the room. Mark's extensive tape and compact disk collection was thrown all over the floor, and books and papers had been removed from the shelves and tossed into the center of the room. "Oh, dear," Cass murmured, wondering, for one silly second, if Herman could be responsible for all this mess.

A hand clamped around her throat and dragged her head painfully backward. Cass's scream was cut off almost the second it started as the grip on her throat tightened. She kicked backward and her high-heeled boot grated against a knee. Her attacker grunted and gave her a violent shove onto the floor. She landed, facedown, in the pile of papers. A hand grabbed her shoulder, and yanked her around. Cass found herself staring into a face completely hidden by a black ski mask.

Cass clawed desperately behind her, found the empty hamster cage and smashed it into the mask, covering her attacker with sawdust shavings and hamster food.

Then the lights went out, and the hand on her was gone. Cass rolled away, scrambled to her feet and dove into the hallway.

"Get down!" barked a voice.

Cass ignored it, the shadows in the hall shifted and a hand snagged her forearm in a bone-jerking yank. Something zinged past her ear, and then she was heaved onto the floor of the closet.

"Stay put!" ordered a familiar American voice.

"Oh no," Cass gasped. "Not again!"

He didn't hang around for chitchat. He slammed the closet door shut, leaving Cass in total darkness, surrounded by Mark's shoes and the coats that had tumbled down around her. She couldn't hear much over the pounding of her heart, but she could make out the sounds of a struggle and another gunshot, followed by footsteps. Cass pushed open the sliding door and raced outside in time to see a car speeding away. She stared after it, then turned back toward the house.

"What in hell was that all about?" demanded a voice.

Cass took one look over her shoulder, saw the enormous figure of Wade Brillings emerging from the darkness and darted toward the open door of Mark's house. She got inside and had the door halfway closed, when he shoved it open, stomped in and kicked it shut behind him. Then he folded his arms and surveyed her with a mixture of exasperation and concern.

Cass backed away from him, rubbing her cold shoulders, trying to make sense of what had just happened. "Wh-what are you doing here?" she stuttered.

"Keeping you from getting shot!" His face and voice were filled with disapproval. "What happened?"

"A burglar." Cass felt the room perform a slow circle around her. "He was choking me...and...he had a gun and..."

"How did you get away from him?"

"I hit him with the hamster cage." The memory made her shudder.

He glowered up the staircase. "Thousand and two," he mumbled.

"What?"

"There's a thousand and one common household items that can be used as weapons. You just discovered number one thousand and two!" His jaw clenched. "What was he after?"

"I—I don't know." She tried to think of something that was missing. "Herman is gone. Mark's, uh, hamster."

"You think that character broke in here to rip off a hamster?"

"He's a very nice hamster." Cass was cold now, so cold she was shivering. "Where did you come from? What . . . ?" Her brain seemed to be working in slow motion, but it finally came up with an explanation. "You followed me?"

"Nope."

"Why . . . uh . . . why were you . . . uh—?"

"Heard you scream," he interrupted. "Figured with your track record you were in the middle of another battle." He glared around the hall. "Turns out I was right!"

Cass watched his features fade in and out of focus. "It's that medallion," she said drearily. "I said I got it from Mark and you came here to beat him up or . . . shoot him or . . . whatever you do to people who return your stuff."

"I wasn't planning—"

"I didn't get it from Mark," Cass sniffed. "I said I did so you would go away, but it wasn't the truth. I found it in the parking lot."

He didn't say a word, just stood there studying her with those hard, cold eyes.

"I am phoning the police now," Cass warned. "That is not a threat. It is just what I am going to do."

"Not just yet." He unfolded his arms and took a step toward her. "First I want to know what's going on here."

"I guess somebody broke in. Will you please—"

"Who is he?"

Cass closed her eyes, pleading for this to be a hallucination of some sort. She flicked up her lashes. Wade Brillings was still there, taking up most of the room in the hallway, his face a scowling mass of bad humor. "His name is Jack Smith," she said, improvising. "He regularly breaks into Mark's house, so we're old friends. You could go threaten him. He lives in, um, Tibet."

"Tibet?" His scowl got worse. "Goddamn it, lady—"

"I gave you a name," Cass interrupted. "I know you won't leave without one. It isn't particularly original, but it's the best I can come up with at the moment." She rubbed her throat where the intruder had tried to choke her. "Will you please leave? If you feel you must frighten me you can come by the store tomorrow and do it then. I'm pretty much scared out today."

"I'm not trying—"

"I'm very sorry I brought back your medallion," Cass went on desperately. "I should have known you weren't a nice person, because a nice person wouldn't hang out in a parking lot with a gun. It's another practical-reality thing, I imagine. I'm terrible at those. Everybody says so."

"Lady—"

"Mark is, too," Cass told him. "He doesn't deserve to be put in front of a firing squad because I found your medallion."

"Wasn't planning on that," Wade drawled. "Firing squads take a hell of a lot of paperwork."

"Do they?" Cass imaged a long four-part form labeled Firing Squad Acquisitions. It seemed to make perfect sense. "Well, um, in that case, you can go away, can't you? There must be at least a hundred thousand people in Calgary you haven't either threatened or rescued, so you really should get started." She staggered away from him and gave her fuzzy head a shake. "I guess you saved me from getting shot again, so I should thank you, although right now I think I might have preferred that to you. Now, go away and never, ever, ever come anywhere near me again."

His lips moved into a crooked smile. "Thought I was invited over to your store tomorrow to scare the crap out of you."

Cass's heart gave a lunge of admiration. That air of controlled masculinity was awfully appealing when accompanied by a smile. "I—I changed my mind," she croaked.

His gaze heated as it raked up and down her body. "Why? You got a date?"

"No, I . . ."

"Why not?" He gestured toward her with one hand. "You're a cute little lady. You must have something going on with someone."

Cass sucked in her bottom lip, startled at this line of questioning. "Not at the moment, but . . ."

"Uh-huh." There was a second of silence, then his voice dropped to a whisky-breath drawl. "Let's start again, Miss Cassandra Lloyd. I'm Commander Wade Brillings. United States Navy."

"Navy?" Cass glanced around the hallway. "You came here on a boat?"

"No, ma'am. I left it at home this trip. I'm teaching a few courses at your military base."

"Really?" Cass put her head to one side. "What do you teach? Intimidation?"

He actually chuckled. "No, honey, I—"

"I didn't have teachers like you, but then again, I studied dress design. They could add a few courses in intimidation, though, because there are times when it would come in handy. Mrs. Hammond and her mustard print is a good example. Perhaps you—"

"Did you hit that fellow, or did you just talk at him until he ran off?"

"I hit him." Her voice was getting rather croaky, probably because her throat hurt. "If talking would have worked, I should have done it at my store and maybe you would have left sooner."

He rubbed his fingertips across his forehead. "How about if I apologize for that? I was mighty suspicious of you, but I've got a feeling you don't know what's going down any more than I do."

"I, uh..."

"Think you'd better have a seat." His eyes were wider, and the cold blue had transformed to a summer warmth that seemed to emanate heat. "You seem a mite shook up."

"I'm not..."

"I should take a look at that neck of yours, too."

Before Cass knew what he was up to, he stretched out an arm and cupped a warm palm around her chin. Gently he bent her head to one side and ran an experimental finger around her throat. "Got you in a neck lock, did he?"

"Is that what it's called?" His hand on her and his detached inspection were making her light-headiness worse. She tried to jerk away, but he had a vice grip on her head that made movement impossible.

He lifted her chin and peered underneath. "Yup. You did well to get away." His tone held respect, his breath, warm against her cold skin, made her shiver. He released her chin. "You're getting some real fancy bruises around there. Let's put some ice on it." He pretty much dragged her into the kitchen and dropped her into a chair.

"I wish you'd go away," Cass said plaintively as the room swayed slightly. "I have to call the police and I..."

"I'm not going anywhere. I can't tolerate being argued with, either, so you might as well sit still and hush up. Right now, we're putting ice on that throat." He pulled on his gloves and opened the freezer compartment of the fridge with one finger. "And I'll be calling the police myself."

# 4

"I DIDN'T GET much of a look at him," Cass explained. She fingered the bruises around her neck and shuddered. "I know he had on a dark-blue down jacket, with storm cuffs. It's about four years old, and it's pretty cheap." She gave Evan an apologetic little smile. "That's all I can remember. It's hard to concentrate on appearances when someone is trying to choke you."

Wade felt the corner of his lip lift in a snarl. He wasn't normally a vengeful sort, but he'd like to get his hands on the creep responsible for those bruises. Good thing Miss Lloyd was a quick thinker. And an equally good thing he'd decided to drop by, in spite of what Cass Lloyd thought.

He looked over at her. She was on his right, perched on the green-and-blue plaid sofa in Mark's living room, with a glass of ice water in her hand. Her face was beginning to regain some color, but her mottled green-and-brown eyes were still wide with shock, and the hand holding the glass trembled slightly. She sure didn't seem like someone experienced in dealing with armed assailants, weapons smugglers or even police asking questions.

Wade glanced across the room at the policeman asking the questions. Evan McCleod was settled into one of the two deep-green armchairs flanking the sofa, his narrow face and pale gray eyes showing nothing of his thoughts. Good thing, too. He'd shared some of those thoughts with Wade when he'd arrived twenty minutes ago, and Wade wasn't partial to hearing any more of them.

Wade hadn't told Evan all the details about his visit to Cass's store—only that he'd received the medallion, dropped by the store to find out where she'd gotten it, then continued on here. Evan hadn't been impressed. Apparently he classed Wade's activities as "conducting your own investigation," although Wade personally considered them more of a reconnaissance mission.

Evan's bad humor hadn't kept him from acting professionally. He and the lab team he'd brought with him had driven up without flashing lights and screaming sirens to announce their arrival. The lab boys were still in the house, digging bullets out of walls and lifting fingerprints off likely looking objects. Wade doubted either of those endeavors would prove worthwhile, though. Orion's crowd wasn't stupid.

If Orion's crowd was involved. Wade was still trying to make up his mind about that. He'd found nothing in Mark Dowling's plain, two-bedroom bungalow to suggest he was anything more than Cass had described him—a computer expert who liked to ski. The photograph Cass had produced of him, showing a brown-haired, rather vague-looking fellow with eyes like hers, had confirmed that impression.

But some of Orion's men were people just like that. Oh, a few were tough characters who could hit a research station, get the goods and get out in less than ten minutes. However, others were innocuous fellows like Cass's cousin, who handed over bribe money to some disgruntled research assistant, got something very secret and very expensive in return and carried it out of the country. Mark Dowling could have an important item in his possession, and could have decided to turn it over to Wade in return for protection.

Wade was positive the man in the black suede jacket was trying to do that very thing. Since he hadn't contacted Wade again, it was fair to assume that Orion's men had found out what he had in mind and were after him.

That man could be Mark Dowling. After all, Dowling had got Cass to return Wade's medallion. Armed men had tried to break into his car and had searched his house. And there was a black suede jacket hanging in his front closet.

Wade turned his attention back to Cass. She had to be the most baffling human being he'd ever encountered. Right now she looked small and helpless and utterly feminine, but less than an hour ago, she'd bashed someone with a hamster cage, then stood in Mark's front hall, facing him down. Her wide-set, camouflage eyes seemed guileless, but her explanation for his medallion's return was questionable. She'd maintained a wary attitude toward him while they were waiting for the police, but every so often, he caught her studying him with undisguised admiration.

And every so often Wade found himself eyeing her exactly the same way. Every time he caught himself doing it, he told himself to stop, but he was having difficulty following his own orders. His reaction to her was unusual for him, and it made him suspicious of her. He didn't know much about womem and it was quite possible she was doing this to him on purpose.

Evan cleared his throat and asked Cass another question. "Can you tell if anything is missing?"

Cass rested back against the sofa cushions. "I still haven't found Mark's hamster, Herman." She peeked at Wade from under the cover of her lashes, then quickly looked away. "I know that man didn't take him, but he is missing."

"I'm...uh...sure he'll turn up," Evan said rather blankly. "Anything else?"

Cass glanced around the room. "It appears everything is here, but it's hard to tell with the place all messed up. Mark owns a lot of computer and stereo equipment. I probably wouldn't notice if some of that was gone." She sipped at the glass of water in her hand and one small fragment of ice slid between her lips. "Mark will have to check when he gets back."

"Of course." Evan made a note. "And when will that be?"

"I'm not sure."

Cass played with the ice, rolling it from one cheek to another, obviously savoring its coolness. Wade watched her covertly, almost feeling the cold against his own cheek. He wrenched his gaze away. It was just a woman drinking water, that's all. Nothing that fascinating about it.

"We should contact Mr. Dowling about this," Evan was saying. "Can you tell me how to reach him?"

Cass gave the ice a long suck before swallowing. "I don't know where he is right now."

"Is there anyone else who would know?"

"His office might." She took another sip of water, and another bit of ice drifted into her mouth. "That's VisTec Computer Consulting. If he's away on business, they might know how to reach him, but if he's skiing, they wouldn't."

Her lips were partly open, giving Wade a glimpse of her pink tongue stroking the ice. He felt beads of sweat break out on his brow, and again ordered himself to cut it out.

Evan sighed heavily. "Where does he usually ski?"

Cass slid the ice to the back of her mouth and swallowed it very slowly, while gesturing vaguely with one hand. "All over."

Wade found his gaze following the gesture. Everything about the woman was colorful, including her vivid pink nail polish. He studied her fingers, noting that the nails were short and all the same length. She wasn't wearing a ring of any sort, and she'd told him she wasn't seeing anyone. Why was that? She had to be close to thirty, and she was certainly attractive. How come she hadn't settled down?

He looked down at his own hands and frowned. He was supposed to be getting information about Dowling, not thinking about Cass Lloyd's marital status. Her answer about Mark's whereabouts had sounded evasive. Was it? Or did she simply not know anything?

Wade couldn't tell. If she were a man, well, he'd be almost positive that the fellow was telling the truth. With her, he wasn't sure.

He tried to call on his other experiences with women, and couldn't think of any. He had no sisters, and his mother had passed away when he was very young. His only brother, Morgan, hadn't married. Wade himself had never been closely involved with a woman. Hell, it had probably been two years since he'd even bothered to sleep with one. It had been a pleasant enough experience, he recalled, and every now and then he got an urge for it, but the older he got, the more infrequent those became.

He watched Cass slide her tongue across her bottom lip, and realized he was darn close to having one of those urges now.

Evan leaned back and studied Cass out of narrow eyes. "When was the last time you spoke with your cousin?"

Cass raised the glass to her lips again, and Wade's muscles clenched.

"Monday. He called me around six and asked me to pick up his car because he had to leave town."

"Does Mark often leave town at such short notice?"

Cass nodded. "Mark always leaves town at short notice." She wrinkled her nose. "He's very clever, but he can be a bit . . . absentminded at times."

"Really?" Evan tapped his fingers together. "You haven't spoken with him since he called?"

She shook her head and took a long drink, and to Wade's discomfort continued to play with the ice.

Evan's tone remained bland. "What about when he gave you Commander Brillings's medallion?"

"He didn't give me that. I . . ." Her voice trailed off, and she looked over at Wade with a confused expression. "You told him about that?"

Wade looked back at her without saying a word. Then the confusion faded into accusation. "You said you didn't have to call the police for help!"

Wade still didn't reply, although mentally he was squirming. He hadn't done anything wrong, damn it! There was no reason for him to feel as though he should crawl back under a rock.

Cass swung around to face Evan. "I don't know what Cap—er, Corporal Brillings told you, but I wasn't trying to blackmail anybody!" She plunked the glass down on the pine coffee table. "I don't do that sort of thing!"

Evan shot Wade a startled, quizzical look, while Cass ranted on. "I don't even know how to blackmail someone. Don't you need a . . . a ransom note or something? And don't you usually do it to a rich person? People in the military don't seem that rich to me. I've got some very wealthy clients with terrible figure flaws whom I'm sure would be much better candidates!"

She stopped for a breath, and Evan took the opportunity get a word in. "I'm not making any sort of accusation," he soothed. "I'm just interested in how the medallion came into your possession."

"Why?" Her voice rose. "You can't possibly think someone did this to Mark's house because of that medallion!"

"No, I—"

"Then why are you asking me about it?" Cass folded her arms protectively across her chest and glared suspiciously at both of them, while the color seeped out of her face. "Mark doesn't know anything about any of this. I'm the one who found it and—"

"And I'm mighty glad you did," Wade said in his slowest, mildest drawl.

It was the only thing he could think of that would stop her going off on one of her little tirades, and it worked far better than he'd expected. Cass's mouth gaped, her cheeks flushed and her gaze softened. "You are?"

"Uh-huh. That medallion has been in my family for a long time. I'd hate to lose it."

"Oh." Cass's flush deepened and her eyes shimmered with a hint of admiration, reminding him of the way she'd looked at him in her store. She lowered her lashes, then raised them and spoke only to him. "The chain is broken. I imagine that's why it fell off in the first place. You need to get it fixed before you wear it again."

The noises of the lab boys seemed to fade away, as did Evan and everything else in the world. There was only Cass and him, alone in the room, looking at each other.

Then Evan broke the spell. "I'd still like to know where you got—"

Wade cut him off. "Don't rightly see why that matters. Cassie is right. That fellow didn't break in here because of my medallion."

Evan's glower was a lot fiercer than Cass's had been, but Wade ignored it. He was concentrating on the expression in Cass's eyes. He needed to find out a lot more from this woman, and he needed to find out if she was telling the truth or not. If he was alone with her, talking to her all nice and friendly, he might find out a lot more than he would if Evan badgered her.

And he wouldn't have to worry about her giving him nasty little glares, or going into a tirade, either.

He turned to Evan. "We about done here? Cassie is still some shook up. Be best if I took her on home."

Cass gave a little gasp, while Evan glowered disapproval. "The lab boys will be another hour or so."

"You don't need Cass here for that, do you?"

Evan's jaw tightened. "Not if Miss Lloyd doesn't object to our being in the house without her, but—"

"You got a problem with that?" Wade asked Cass.

She shook her head. "No, but . . . you don't have to take me home. I can . . ."

"Least I can do, ma'am," Wade said easily. "I gave you one hell of a scare earlier. Like to make up for it."

"Oh," Cass said again. "Well. Thank you. That's very kind, but I have Mark's car and . . ."

"We'll take it," Wade decided immediately. "One of Evan's folks can drive mine over when they're done here." He lifted an eyebrow at Evan. "All right with you?"

Evan considered it for a long moment, then gave in. "Fine." He shoved himself out of the chair. "You're free to leave, Miss Lloyd. I'll contact you if I have any more questions." He caught Wade's eye and gestured toward the hallway. "I'd like a word with you."

"Bet you would," Wade grunted. He followed Evan out into the hall.

Evan stopped just around the corner, out of view of the living room, and folded his arms. "When we play good cop, bad cop, I like to be the good cop."

"I'm not playing anything," Wade denied. "I'm just seeing that the little lady gets home safely."

Evan's look was one of pure disbelief. "Uh-huh."

Wade rubbed the back of his neck. "You were getting her all riled up, Evan."

"I was trying to get some answers!"

"Well, you were doing a mighty poor job of it."

Evan's eyes narrowed. "So you're going to take her home and see if you can do better? Is that it?"

Wade winced. "I'll have a little friendly conversation with her, that's all."

"Friendly, huh?" Evan studied Wade closely. "What was all that blackmail talk about?"

Wade shrugged philosophically. "Hard to say what's going on in her mind."

"It's your mind I'm concerned about." Evan's gaze sharpened. "You wouldn't, uh . . ."

Wade didn't appreciate the suspicion on the other man's face. "I'm taking her home and I'm talking to her," he snarled. "That's all there is to it." He softened his tone. "I'm an American naval officer, Inspector. She's safe with me."

Evan studied him for another moment, then capitulated. "Okay. I'll pick you up at her place myself when I'm done here. And if she says anything I ought to know, I want to hear about it. Got it?"

Wade considered this and nodded.

Evan pursed his lips, shrugged and wandered toward the back of the house.

Wade returned to the living room. Cass was on her hands and knees, crawling around on the floor, a bright splash of blue-and-green against the dark carpet. "You still looking for that hamster?" he guessed.

She glanced up over her shoulder. "I can't leave until I find him." She used the sofa to push herself to her feet and produced a small, wary smile. "It could take a little while. There's no reason for you to wait around. I'm sure you've got other things to do, and—"

"Can't think of anything I'd rather be doing," Wade interjected. "And I don't want to hear any more arguments about it."

"Oh, that's right," Cass murmured. A small smile played across her lips. "You can't tolerate being argued with."

"That's right, honey. Now, let's find that hamster." He thought for a second and gestured toward the dining area at the far end of the room. "He's probably in there."

Cass's forehead furrowed, making her nose wrinkle. "How do you know?"

"First rule of tracking is, think like your quarry. A hamster doesn't want to sit around under a sofa. He'd be more interested in eating."

She looked skeptical. "Really?"

"Uh-huh." Wade strode toward the dining area, with Cass trailing behind him. Sure enough, a brown furry creature with round eyes was crouched beside a table leg. "I'd guess that's Herman."

"It is!" Cass sounded impressed. She knelt down and studied the hamster. "Hi, Herman. Did that horrible man scare you?"

Wade crouched beside her and watched her watch the hamster. Her pupils were still a bit dilated, and in this light they seemed more green than brown. She had a faint, feminine scent of perfume, not overpowering, but the kind that sneaks up on a person. He motioned toward the hamster. "You going to catch that animal or are we going to sit here and stare at him?"

She lifted a browny gold eyebrow. "I don't know how to catch a hamster. Do you?"

"Move slowly," Wade advised. "Don't want to scare him."

Cass eyed Herman, then batted her eyes at Wade. "Maybe you could..."

Wade stood up and backed away. "If you're suggesting I catch that critter, you can forget it. I found him. The rest is up to you."

Cass tilted her head to one side. "Why?"

Wade considered his response and decided on the truth. "I don't pick up rodents unless I have to."

Her gaze traveled slowly up to meet his. When it did, all traces of wariness were gone, leaving the open admiration that he'd seen when he'd first stepped into her store. He'd given her the right answer, Wade decided. Apparently women liked to know a man had a few vulnerabilities.

"Are you afraid of hamsters, Lieutenant?" she breathed.

An almost forgotten heat began pooling in Wade's groin, and he fought it down. "I'm fairly confident the critter isn't going to shoot me, but I'd rather not pick him up. And how about if you call me 'Wade'? Every time you open your mouth, I get a new rank."

"I've never known anyone in the military before," Cass explained. "They don't come into my dress shop too often. They should, though. Some of those uniforms could use help." She eyed him up and down, as if mentally dressing him, and her tongue licked her bottom lip. Then, with a quick shake of her head, she began creeping toward the animal. "Come here, Herman. Don't run off, okay?"

Wade watched her back view as she moved along on hands and knees. This was going to work out just fine. He was positive that now that she'd relaxed, he'd have no problem finding out what he wanted to know.

Right now, though, the only thing he was wondering about was the taste of that bottom lip of hers.

CASS SAT very straight in the passenger seat of Mark's Camaro, holding the hamster cage on her lap and watching Wade's wide hands curl around the steering wheel. He'd warmed up the car before escorting her and Herman out of the house, although Cass felt that had been unnecessary. The heat from his body seemed to fill the interior as much as the air blasting from the car heater.

Now she was beginning to wonder if being alone with him was such a good idea. He'd saved her a couple of times, and he'd been very nice to her at Mark's place, but she didn't know why he'd told the police about that medallion. "Is that policeman a friend of yours?" she asked.

Wade glanced at her out of the corner of his eye. "Inspector McCleod? I wouldn't call him that, no."

Cass took a deep breath. "Then why did you tell him about your medallion?"

"Didn't have much choice." Wade took another look at her. "He'd already pegged you as the brunette from the parking lot last night. He wanted to know how I'd tracked you down."

"You told him about that, *too?*"

"Uh-huh."

"Oh." Cass turned her head and stared out the side window. She'd been worried he'd get in trouble if she called the police, and he'd gone and done it himself. There was obviously a whole bunch of reality stuff going on that she didn't understand.

"Why didn't *you* call the police on that?" Wade asked after a moment.

"I didn't see any point." Cass stared down at the hamster cage on her lap. "I couldn't identify anybody. And . . . and I thought it might get you in trouble." She took a quick peek at his profile. "I thought that might be why you left."

"You figured right," he confirmed. "Us military folks aren't supposed to go around shooting up parking lots, especially in a foreign country."

"Oh." Cass was still confused. "Why were you there with a gun then?"

"Just happened to be by." He glanced over. "You?"

"Oh, I was just picking up this car. Mark left it there for me."

Wade scowled. "You shouldn't have been there so late all on your lonesome. That's just asking for trouble."

"I didn't mean to be there so late. It's just the way it turned out."

"How's that?"

"Mark called around six and asked me to pick up his car. I sort of . . . forgot until later." Cass waited for a moment, but he didn't say anything about her being too absentminded. She relaxed back against the seat. "I never thought about anyone trying to steal it."

"Maybe they weren't," Wade said thoughtfully. "Maybe they were after something inside."

"There wasn't anything inside." She watched Wade's thigh shift as he eased on the brakes. "Just a bag of hamster stuff and a jacket."

"What sort of jacket?"

His tone sounded casual, but there was an alert air about him, Cass noted. "Just an old black suede jacket," she said quickly. "It wasn't worth breaking into the car for. Besides, I don't think they could have seen it from outside. It was on the floor of the back seat."

"That so?" Wade took an over-the-shoulder glance at the back. "It still in here?"

"No. I put it in Mark's house." She remembered the image she'd received when she'd hung it up. "It doesn't belong to him, though. I wonder—"

"How do you know it isn't his?"

"Uh . . ." Cass realized he wouldn't believe her if she tried to explain. "I've just never seen him wear it, that's all."

"Huh." Wade's eyebrows came down and he settled into a brooding silence.

Cass studied his profile, but it was impossible to tell what he was thinking. His face was as expressionless as when she'd first met him. She wondered if he practiced that blank look in the mirror, and tried not to giggle at the mental image of him intimidating his own reflection. "Do you live alone?" she asked impulsively.

"Nope."

Cass's heart gave a thump of disappointment, then rose as he continued.

"Most of the time I live with a few hundred other men."

"Oh." Cass watched as he changed lanes. There was a no-nonsense, in-charge aura around him, even when he was doing something simple like driving the car. Heavens, he hadn't skidded once, although the side streets were glazed with ice and treacherous. The car even did what it was told. "You're, uh, not married then?"

"Nope." He glanced over at her. "You?"

"No."

"Why not?"

"What?" Cass asked, startled.

He stopped the car at a red light and faced her. "Why aren't you married?"

"It just, d-didn't happen yet," Cass stuttered. "Why aren't you?"

"Don't run into a lot of women in my line of work."

Cass rubbed her tongue across her lip. "And that's teaching?"

"Teaching...advising...a few other things, as well." His teeth flashed under the streetlights when he grinned. "And I don't teach intimidation techniques, either, in case you're still wondering."

"You should," Cass murmured. "You're very good at it."

"That so?" He peered at her through the darkness. "You still intimidated?"

She was a bit, but she wasn't going to admit it. "Not really," she said, instead. "Anyone who's scared of a hamster can't be all that fierce."

The light changed. "Keep it to yourself," he grumbled. "Stuff like that can ruin a man's reputation."

As if he had to worry about that! Cass bet half the navy was intimidated by him. "Turn left at the next light. What do you teach?"

"Surveillance, unarmed combat, counterterrorism, survival techniques.... And a few other subjects."

Just the sort of thing a man like him should teach. "But you don't live in Calgary?"

"Nope. I'm here on an exchange program. Got another three weeks left."

"Three weeks," Cass repeated. "Where do you live then? When you're not here?"

He shrugged. "Depends on what day you're talking about. I don't generally stay in one place too long."

"Oh." That fitted with his image all right. "You take the next left, down the back alley. My house is the fourth one. There's a parking space at the back."

As soon as he turned down the alley, Cass started to get nervous. It was an older area and there were no streetlights, just tall trees and high fences. Wade drove cautiously, moving his head in a slow appraisal of the area, which made her even more jumpy.

Cass pointed out her parking spot and he stopped the car.

"Stay put," he ordered. "I'll check your house and turn on some lights. Give me your key."

Cass hesitated. Suddenly this didn't seem like a good idea at all. She was all alone with someone who'd pretty much threatened her earlier. He was awfully big and she really didn't know him. What on earth had possessed her to come with him? Now he was going to go into her house and . . .

She put a hand on the door handle. "That's, uh, fine. Really. Thank you for bringing me home. I'm sure you don't want to wait around here, so why—"

"Oh, for christsake!" He grabbed her wrist and held her in place. Then he stuck a hand into his jacket pocket and pulled out the medallion. "You see this?"

Cass's heart gave a giant leap of alarm as she stared at it. "I wasn't . . . uh . . . trying to blackmail you. Honestly. I don't—"

"I don't plan on ever having another conversation about it with you." He released her wrist and replaced the medallion in his pocket. "I'm mighty grateful to get it back. That's all that needs to be said."

Cass blinked at him. "Oh. Well . . . uh . . ."

"Now, do you think you can stop being so goddamn jumpy and let me secure the place?"

# 5

WADE BRILLINGS was exactly the touch her living room needed.

Cass sat in a white wicker chair and silently admired his masculine form sprawled in the center of the matching wicker sofa. His blue jeans and olive green sweater didn't really coordinate with her fuchsia, pale pink and white decorating scheme, but he added a male touch that the room had previously lacked.

Cass hadn't exactly invited him in. Before she could issue an invitation or offer him something to drink, he'd removed his jacket, found a beer in her fridge and even poured her a glass of juice. Then he'd announced they'd sit in the living room and marched into it.

He studied his surroundings with great care, then focused on her. Was it her imagination, or did his stunning blue eyes show the same admiration she was feeling for him?

He took a large swallow of beer, then gestured around the room with the can of beer in his hand. "This what you had in mind when you suggested doing something about our uniforms?"

Cass immediately envisioned a couple of hundred Wade Brillings clones, dressed in white, fuchsia and pale pink. "Not exactly," she murmured. She'd rather have a couple of hundred men like him dressed in nothing but white socks and white T-shirts. "What color is your living room?"

"I don't generally have one."

"Oh." Cass couldn't imagine a life-style that involved not having a living room. "You mean you don't have a place of your own?"

He shrugged as if it were totally unimportant. "Depends where I'm stationed." He raised the can again. "How do you happen to be using Mark's car? There something wrong with yours?"

Cass focused on his forearms. He'd shoved up the sleeves of his green sweater, giving her a good view of them. As she'd suspected, they were covered with that sandy-red hair, and looked as strong and muscular as the rest of him. "I don't have a car," she said through suddenly dry lips. "Every time I save up some money, I find something I want more." She waited for a second, but he didn't say anything about her being too extravagant. "I don't really need one, anyway," she added. "Mark lends me his whenever he's out of town."

"That happen a lot?"

"Uh-huh." Cass was staring at his arms again. "VisTec is always sending him places and he skis a lot, too."

"How about yourself? You travel much?"

"What? Oh. No, not really. I never can save up enough money for that."

Wade's eyes narrowed slightly. He motioned toward the glass shelves in the corner. "Looks as if you've been a few places."

Cass wrenched her gaze away from his arm. "Oh, those are from Mark. He usually buys me an ornament or something when he's away. The troll is from Norway, that silver bell is from Aspen, the sand sculpture is from Arizona, that little red sports car is from Detroit—"

"When was he there?" Wade interrupted, with no particular expression.

Cass considered it. "Last March I think."

Wade stared at it for a moment. "Decent of him."

"Oh, Mark's very nice," Cass agreed eagerly. "He's always doing things for me. As a matter of fact, my parents wouldn't have let me come here at all if Mark wasn't here."

"That so?" Wade raised an eyebrow. "You're not from around here then?"

"Oh, no. My parents' farm is near Eaglesham—that's about twelve hundred kilometers north of here." Cass settled back in the chair as she talked. "My family was really against my coming here. They didn't like the idea of my being so far away."

"Why not? You seem quite able to handle yourself."

"Oh." Cass flushed at the compliment. "Well ... uh ... my family didn't think so. I'm the only girl and my brothers are much older. They're a bit overprotective and they didn't think I could handle living in a city."

"Probably never seen you in action with a hamster cage," Wade said, straight-faced.

"I guess not." Cass was entranced by the lazy humor in his eyes, and had to force herself to concentrate on the conversation. "Anyway, I talked to Mark about it. He's my mother's sister's son, and we sort of grew up together, although he's four years older than me. He was already living here. He promised my parents he'd look after me."

"What was he doing here?"

"Computer stuff," Cass said vaguely. "I'm not too sure. He keeps explaining it, but it's sort of beyond me."

"I'm no hell at it, either," Wade admitted.

"Really?" It was difficult to believe there was anything this man wasn't good at.

Wade held up a hand, with the fingers spread wide apart. "Hands are too big for those bitty keyboards."

Cass took in the size of the hand he was holding up and her mouth went dry again. "I, uh, guess they would be."

He dropped his hand, and Cass followed it with her gaze, enjoying the way it looked spread out on his thigh.

"Mark's friends all computer types, as well?"

Cass focused back on his face. "Most of them are, I guess. I don't know many of them. He's introduced me to a few. They're very nice, but I can never understand what they're talking about and they have very boring taste in clothes. Mark does, too, but I usually shop with him." She put her head to one side and examined

Wade's outfit. "I suppose the navy chooses your clothes for you."

"They have an opinion about the uniforms," Wade agreed. "I generally choose the rest myself." He glanced at his apparel. "There something wrong with them?"

"Oh, no. They're fine, although I would have guessed you'd prefer brown."

"That so?" One corner of his lip curled up. "You spend a lot of time thinking about clothes, do you?"

"It's what I do," Cass said rather defensively. "I design clothes for people. You probably spend a lot of time thinking about—" she wrinkled her nose mischievously "—intimidation."

"Always at the back of my mind," he agreed solemnly. He raised the beer can again. "Doesn't this cousin of yours have a girlfriend to pick out his clothes for him?"

"Hmmm? Oh ... uh ..." Cass shook her head. "Not right now. He works with women, but I guess he doesn't hang out with them a whole lot. I think he gets so involved with his computer stuff that he doesn't notice they *are* women. Is that what happens to you?"

"Wouldn't say that." Wade's tone was a deep drawl. "I'm pretty good at telling the difference between a ship and a woman." He motioned toward the family picture hanging on her wall. "Who are all those folks?"

IT WAS half an hour later when Cass heard the sounds of a car pulling up in front of her house. She glanced at her watch, surprised at how much time had passed.

Darn. She'd wanted to find out more about him, but she had done most of the talking. That was unusual—most men seemed to want to talk about themselves, or their work.

She had no sooner heard the car engine than Wade was at the window, taking a cautious peek between the slats of the venetian blinds.

"My ride," he announced after a moment.

Cass followed him to the front door and watched while he put on his jacket and boots. He must have a body temperature well above normal, she decided. The heat seemed to seep from him and spread surround her. She tucked in her bottom lip.

For a moment he gazed at her mouth, then his eyes slid up to meet hers. "Thanks for the beer."

"You're welcome." Cass shifted her weight from foot to foot. "Thank you for saving me—both times. And for bringing me home and turning on the lights." She giggled a little nervously. "I'll probably leave them on all night and think I hear burglars."

"I've got a solution for that." Although the rest of his face showed nothing, his blue eyes were now filled with hot summer fire.

"What?" Cass murmured.

"This." Wade took a step closer and framed her face with his palms. Then he dropped his head and moved his tongue slowly along her bottom lip.

Cass gave a little whimper and put her hands on his shoulders to hold herself up. He tilted her head back. "Open your mouth, baby. I want a taste of that, too."

Cass's lips dropped open all by themselves. His tongue probed inside, then came out to her bottom lip again. She stood there, clutching him, her head held backward by his hands as he thoroughly and methodically nibbled and licked and sucked and tasted every part of her mouth.

He lifted his face for a breath, kept her head trapped in his hands and started again. No other part of his body touched her—just his lips, and his hands and his tongue. It wasn't really a kiss, Cass thought hazily. It was more like an exploration, and my, oh my, it felt delicious.

He pulled her bottom lip into his mouth one last time, abruptly dropped his hands and stepped back to survey her. "That take your mind off burglars?"

"W-what?"

He grinned with smug satisfaction. "Guess it did."

Before she could respond, he was gone, leaving her staring at the closed door.

WADE CLIMBED into Evan's car, feeling extremely satisfied with himself. He'd found out everything he wanted to know, and he'd even had a taste of Cass Lloyd's bottom lip. Not bad, for someone out of practice.

He leaned back in the seat and allowed himself a couple of seconds to savor the lingering taste of her. It had been a while since he'd kissed a woman. He'd sort of forgotten the softness of their lips, the warm moistness of their mouth. The sensations it created in his body.

That was why he'd enjoyed the experience so much, Wade rationalized. He'd ignored that part of his life for a long time. That was probably why he'd been so distracted by her, too. He needed to take control again—get a little more exercise, perhaps. He'd been sitting behind a desk or standing in a classroom for too long.

Maybe he shouldn't have kissed her. Wade shrugged that off. No reason not to. She'd been tormenting him all evening with the invitation in her eyes. It hadn't done any harm, and it probably *had* taken her mind off burglars. He felt another smug smile cross his lips. She'd enjoyed the experience as much as he had.

Actually, he'd enjoyed every moment he'd spent with her. He'd never been much good at idle chitchat, but getting her to talk had been easy. Hell, she'd pretty much interrogated herself. He grinned as he recalled her odd bits of conversation. Her mind was as scattered as the feminine articles strewn around the house. Wade was an orderly man himself—had to be in his occupation—but he'd gotten a kick out of seeing unmatched high-heeled shoes, bottles of nail polish and pieces of clothing scattered through every room.

Wade had seen every room, too. He'd taken a thorough look around while he was checking the place for her. A person's habitat told a lot, and Cass's was no exception. Her narrow, three-bedroom bungalow was very clean, rather untidy and extremely colorful. Lots of bright pink, yellow, mauve, all put together against a brilliant white background. It wasn't the sort of thing he would have chosen, but . . .

He watched Evan pull away from the curb and scowled. He didn't have to think about decorating schemes. He lived in officers' quarters for short-term assignments, and found himself a furnished place to rent for longer ones. He didn't worry about what color they were or how they looked. As long as the bed was fairly comfortable and he had a place for his gear, he was fine.

He didn't need a lot of space, either. He didn't have a whole lot of personal possessions—they weren't worth the time it took to pack them up.

He hadn't wasted time tonight, either. He'd found out more than he'd expected, just by listening to Cass talk. He was positive now that she was telling the truth. She'd told him too much too readily to be a person with something to hide.

Too bad he couldn't say the same for her cousin.

"Well?" Evan demanded.

Wade leaned back against the cold upholstery and took a breath. "Dowling's our boy, all right."

"I CAN'T GET a warrant for Dowling's arrest," Evan insisted. "What am I going to charge him with? Trying to steal his own car? Breaking into his own house? What?"

Wade glared across the front seat of the car. He'd told Evan everything he'd found out, and he'd even put it together the way he saw it. Yet Evan was still having difficulty grasping the situation. "I'm not suggesting you do anything," Wade said, trying to sound reasonable. "I just want the man found before the rest of Orion's crew get their hands on him. If they know he was planning on talking to me, they won't be real nice to him."

"We don't even know Orion is involved." Evan paused meaningfully. "Unless Miss Lloyd told you something different."

"Cass wouldn't know Orion if he walked into her house." He wouldn't be the pink-and-mauve-and-yellow type at all. Just as Wade wasn't.

"I tend to agree with you." Evan scratched absently at his temple. "I'm not convinced her cousin would, either."

Wade ground his teeth with exasperation. "Mark told me he was working for Orion when he phoned."

"You don't *know* that was Mark Dowling."

"I know it was a fellow who owned a black suede jacket! I know he was going to be at the Brentwood rapid-transit parking lot Monday night. Dowling fits the bill! Cass found his jacket in that car and—"

"I thought she told you it wasn't his jacket."

"She did," Wade admitted. "Doesn't mean a thing, though. Cassie is just trying to protect Mark, that's all. Same goes for my medallion. Dowling had to have told her it was mine. I gave her a scare in her store, and she changed her story to protect him. She doesn't know what she's protecting him from, but she's doing it."

It was foolish of her, of course, but Wade could understand it. In some strange way, he even admired her for it. And in an even stranger way, he almost envied Mark Dowling for having someone like Cassie who cared enough to protect him.

"Did you ask her about it?" Evan asked.

"No! There's no point."

"There might be." Evan's eyes narrowed thoughtfully. "Maybe I should have another talk with her. Find out if she knows something more."

Wade didn't care for the idea of Evan giving Cass the third degree. "How about if we just find Dowling," he suggested. "Then we can ask him."

Evan shifted behind the steering wheel. "What's this 'we' stuff? You're not proposing to do a little investigating of your own, are you?"

Wade didn't bother to deny it. "You folks got a law against my asking a few questions?"

"No, we don't. But I don't want you doing it. This is a police matter, Commander. There's no reason for the American navy—"

"Dowling could have something we want," Wade interrupted. "If he's the one who called me, then there's a good chance he's got some hot little item on him. I figure that's why those characters were breaking into his car and his house. He must have taken something from Orion, and they're trying to get it back. Since he contacted me, it could be something that was lifted from us."

Evan stroked his chin. "You folks missing something?"

"My *folks* don't generally call me up every time something goes astray. But there's a good chance Dowling has something, and I want to know what it is."

Evan was silent for a moment. "I'm afraid you'll just have to wait for me to tell you."

Wade started to give his opinion about that and Evan held up a hand. "Look, Commander, I appreciate your position. However, we don't know what's happening here. It could be nothing. It could be that your suspicions are correct. Or it could be an elaborate setup to get even with you. You mentioned you'd had run-ins with Orion before."

"That was years ago!"

"Maybe Orion has a long memory," Evan said meaningfully. "We don't want anything happening to you in our country."

Wade frowned at this. What was it with these Canadians? The military was supposed to protect people, not the other way around. "Nothing is going to happen to me," he snapped.

"It won't if you're on the base."

Wade clenched his teeth. "I want the man found, Evan."

"How about if you leave that up to me?" Evan's tone indicated this was more than a suggestion. "I'm with the RCMP—we always get our man. I'll run a check on

Dowling. I'll find out where he is and what he's doing. When I do, I'll give you a call."

Wade considered it. Evan had a good point. This wasn't his country, and he had no formal orders to do anything more than cooperate with the local police. Still, he felt some responsibility for Orion being on the loose. He wanted the man captured and his little operation halted. For that to happen, though, Wade needed to talk to the man who had contacted him, the man in the black suede jacket. Wade was convinced that man was Mark Dowling. Dowling had to be found, before Orion's group got their hands on him and made sure he didn't talk to anyone ever again. Cassie would be very unhappy if that happened.

He thought about her again, about the way she tasted, the way she'd looked at him. "What about Cassie?" he asked. "Orion's folks could come after her, looking for Dowling."

Evan sighed impatiently. "We'll handle Miss Lloyd. Go back to the base and forget all about this."

Wade considered it for another minute. He didn't want to promise to do something he wasn't going to do. But there was no logical reason for him to insist on being involved. The RCMP were very competent. They didn't need him to find Dowling, and they didn't need him to watch Cass, either.

It would be best if he did go back to the base and get on with what he was supposed to be doing. His last session started next week. He had notes to review, training logistics to settle . . . all sorts of details to keep him occupied. There was no reason to concern himself with this until Dowling was found.

He gave Cass one last thought then pushed her out of his mind. There was no need for him to go on thinking about her, either.

# 6

"DEAR HEAVEN," Lydia murmured. She dropped into the chair behind her desk in a swirl of black and white, her dark eyes filled with astonishment. "You mean this navy fellow just showed up out of nowhere and—"

"That's right," Cass said quickly. She took a neat bite of the chocolate, pink-sprinkled doughnut in her hand and followed it with a swallow of coffee. There were lots of things about last night that she hadn't told Lydia, including Wade's appearance at the store and the whole mess about how she knew the medallion belonged to him. Those were things she didn't even want to think about, much less describe to her terribly practical business partner. Instead, she'd started the story with her arrival at Mark's house and the subsequent action there. Now she wanted to conclude the tale, before Lydia asked any difficult questions. "Then Wa—er, Captain Brillings called the police. They came and he took me home." Then he'd kissed the daylights out of her, but Cass didn't feel like sharing that, either.

Lydia's voice sharpened. "*He* took you home?"

"Yes." Cass took another sip of coffee and searched for a way to change the subject. "And then Herman kept me up half the night."

"Herman?"

"Mark's hamster," Cass explained. "He was really upset. He kept running around in his wheel and it makes the most awful squeak—like fingernails on a blackboard. I finally had to take it out. Herman was ever so cross at me." Cass finished her doughnut. "He cheered up when I gave him that new toy Mark bought him."

She'd forgotten all about the gray box she'd found in Mark's car until very late at night. When she'd pulled it out of her purse, she'd wondered about it again. It didn't look like much of a hamster toy, but Herman had been delighted. He'd immediately set to work covering it with shavings. By this morning, nothing could be seen of it. "He's quite a clever little hamster," she added.

"That's, uh, splendid," Lydia said, and cleared her throat. "This navy fellow—what was he doing at Mark's place? Is he a friend of Mark's?"

"No." Cass stared down into her cup. "He... uh...just happened by." She realized she'd used one of Wade's expressions and smiled. There was a lot to be learned from a practical person like him—one was how to answer a question without really saying anything. She took a peek at Lydia, who was tapping the end of her pen thoughtfully on the top of her desk.

"What about that thing in the parking lot the other night?" Lydia asked suddenly. "Did you mention that to the police?"

Cass searched for another evasion. "It . . . uh . . . sort of came up."

"Do they think there's any connection—"

"I have no idea what the police think," Cass interrupted. She set her cup down on her workbench. "They never tell you that. They just ask you all sorts of questions that don't make any sense."

"Oh, dear." Lydia was instantly sympathetic. "They didn't give you a bad time, did they?"

"Not really," Cass said after a moment. She wiped doughnut crumbs off her peacock-blue jumpsuit and sighed. "At least they didn't laugh at me. They were all wearing that dull gray color, though. Where on earth do you think they buy it?"

"I have no idea," Lydia murmured vaguely.

Cass drained her coffee cup. "If I ever have to talk to one again, I think I'll ask. That way, I'll know where not to shop."

Lydia's lips twitched. "You do that, dear. Listen, do you think it might be a good idea to give Mark a call? He might need to contact his insurance company."

"I didn't think of that," Cass admitted. "I guess I could phone his office and see if they know where he is."

"I think you should." Lydia began to push herself up, then sat back down. "What's this navy fellow like? Is he married?"

"Wade? He's not married, no." Cass looked down at her workbench. The pattern she'd started for Sue Hammond's dress was there, exactly where she'd left it last night. It seemed like so long ago that Cass could hardly remember what she'd been doing with it. "He's a nice man, Lydia. Tall. Big. And he's got the loveliest eyes—sort of a cross between periwinkle blue and cobalt blue. And he has this interesting way of talking without moving his lips. He's got very good taste in clothes, too. Nothing flashy, but he knows what suits him." She picked up her sketchbook and began thumbing through it.

"You'll have to bring him around here. I'd like to meet him."

Cass found the sketch she'd made of Sue Hammond's dress and studied it. "I don't imagine I'll be seeing him again."

"Why not?" Lydia asked. "He sounds interesting and . . ."

"Oh, he is interesting," Cass acknowledged. "He's the most interesting man I've met in ages." She set her sketchbook down. "And the old, impractical me would make sure she saw him again. But the new, improved me realizes that would not be a good idea. Lydia, he doesn't even have a living room. I mean, how practical can you get?"

"He's in the navy, dear. I don't imagine . . ."

"That's right!" Cass agreed. "Think how down to earth those people are! They couldn't go around forgetting what time their boat left or not washing their gun, could they?" She picked up her sketchbook again. "Besides, I like him far too much."

"Most people do date people they like," Lydia noted. "And I'm sure he likes you. After all, he's a man, he's not married and he's met you."

Cass thought of that hot good-night kiss and sighed regretfully. "Oh, he likes me well enough now, I imagine. But it wouldn't take him long to find out all the things wrong with me. And think how upset I'd be then! It's bad enough when someone I don't like tells me how impractical or how irresponsible I am." She shuddered at the thought of Wade Brillings listing her faults. "I'd feel just . . . terrible."

Lydia sighed with impatience. "Oh, for heaven sakes, Cass, you can't go around rejecting every man you like just because of Charlie!"

"It has nothing to do with Charlie." Cass stared down at the book in her hand. "It's men in general and Wade in particular. I'm not going to date someone I like this much. Besides, I don't imagine he'll call me anyway. A practical person like him has probably found a number of things wrong with me all ready."

HUGH RIGEL LOOKED like that hamster Cass was so concerned about.

Wade noticed the similarity as soon as the innocuous little man wandered hesitantly into his office. He had the same round brown eyes, same round face, same round body. Not as much hair, though. Rigel was loosing his, although what he had was brown and kind of furry looking. Wade had no problem picturing the fellow crouched underneath Mark's dining room table, staring around with wary bewilderment.

The notion annoyed him. It had been a good twelve hours since he'd last seen Cass. He'd mentally reviewed every piece of information he'd gotten from her, analyzed it for clues and filed it away in his memory. There was no reason for him to keep thinking about her.

But he couldn't seem to stop. If he didn't concentrate on pushing her out of his mind, she'd be there in some form or other. He'd find himself chuckling over odd bits of conversation. He'd suddenly wonder why a chair was whatever color it was. Or he'd encounter one of the females on the base and drift off thinking about Cass's eyes, or her hair, or the feel of her mouth under his. Now he was even thinking about her hamster!

Wade gave the phone a good hard glare. Evan hadn't called him yet. Did that mean they hadn't found Dowling, or was he being purposefully kept in the dark? He hoped it was the latter—if the entire police department couldn't track down Dowling in twelve hours, it had to mean the man was staying out of sight on purpose. That fact alone would indicate Wade had been right about Mark.

He should be happy about being right, but this time, he'd rather be wrong. Cass would be upset if her cousin disappeared from her life. That's what would happen. Wade had already contacted his superiors about the situation, and they were fully prepared to offer Dowling a place to hide out in return for testimony against Orion. The RCMP were probably thinking the same thing. No matter who he dealt with, there was no way Dowling would be staying in Calgary.

Then who was going to keep an eye on the little lady?

Wade pushed the concern out of his mind. That wasn't his problem, damn it!

He made a valiant attempt to focus his attention on his visitor. He had no idea who Hugh Rigel was or what the man wanted. He'd just shown up at the gate asking to see Commander Brillings. Wade had agreed, hoping Rigel was somehow connected with Dowling. Now that he'd seen the man, Wade didn't think that was much of a possibility.

Rigel had a manner very reminiscent of Herman—still and kind of watchful. Wade's brain flashed an image of Cass perched on the edge of Mark's sofa, messing around with ice cubes, and he gritted his teeth. "What can I do for you, Mr. Rigel?"

Rigel's dark gaze flitted around the office before settling on Wade. "I'm, uh, with Thorndyke and Howell Electronic Industries?" He passed over a business card.

Wade examined it. Hugh Rigel, Marketing Manager, Thorndyke and Howell Electronic Industries. It didn't ring a bell. He gave Rigel an inquiring look. "Uh-huh?"

Rigel shifted uneasily. "Are you familiar with our company?"

Wade shook his head. "Can't say that I am, no. Should I be?"

"Not necessarily." Rigel coughed discreetly into his hand. "It's a rather awkward situation, Commander. You see, I found your name in the appointment book of an associate of mine and . . . well, I'm not sure how well you know him or—"

"What's this fellow's name?" Wade interrupted.

Rigel hesitated, and his round eyes seemed to bore into Wade's. "Karl Leros."

Wade considered it for a moment. "Never heard of him."

Rigel's shoulders dropped, almost as if he were relieved. "I see." He started to rise. "Well then, there's no reason for me to . . ."

Wade held up a hand. "Hang on a minute. What's this all about? This Leros fellow claiming he knows me, or—"

"Oh no, sir, nothing like that." Rigel settled back down. "It was just difficult to tell from—" he swallowed "—from Karl's notes if you were a personal friend or simply a prospective customer." He coughed, obviously very ill at ease. "I thought I should speak to you personally about it just in case you, uh, happened to be . . . the former."

Wade studied him for a moment, then suddenly got it. "Something happen to this Leros fellow?" he guessed.

"Yes." Rigel nodded sorrowfully. "It was a car accident." Again he studied Wade.

Wade rubbed the back of his neck. "When did this happen?"

Rigel blinked ferociously. "Late Monday night. It's a terrible tragedy. Karl was a very decent person." He cleared his throat once more. "I'm, uh, calling on his friends and associates who might not have heard and . . ."

"And my name was in his appointment book?"

"That's right." Rigel rubbed a hand across his brow. "You see, one of our products is a line of electronic simulation equipment. The Canadian Armed Forces is one of our customers, and we have a few European clients, as well, but we have yet to expand into the U.S. I imagine Karl was hoping to interest you in our products."

Wade nodded without speaking. There were a lot of companies eager to tap into the military market.

"If you are, I could have another of our salesmen contact you," Rigel went on. He snapped open his briefcase. "Or I could leave you some of our brochures...."

"Why don't you do that?" Wade suggested. "I'm not the right person to talk to, but I'll pass them on." He took the glossy brochures Rigel produced and set them on his desk.

Rigel got to his feet and studied Wade again. Then he held out a hand. "Well, thank you, Commander. I'm sorry to have bothered you. I just thought I should contact Karl's friends in person. It, uh, seemed like the right thing to do."

"Decent of you," Wade grunted. He watched the man walk out the door, quickly and nervously. Christ, the man even moved like Herman. Not surprising, considering the reason he was here.

Or was his associate's death the real reason Rigel was here? There was something about the way that man had looked at him that made Wade wonder.

He was probably being overly suspicious. Still, it didn't hurt to check. Maybe Karl Leros had been wearing a black suede jacket when he died.

Besides, it gave him an excuse to phone Evan.

"I DIDN'T CALL, because I have nothing to say," Evan said defensively. "All reports say that Mark Dowling is a fine, upstanding citizen. Hell, he doesn't even have a parking ticket."

Wade scowled at the phone. "That's just the sort Orion likes. No record." He waited for a moment, but Evan didn't respond. "You haven't found him yet?"

Evan hesitated. "No, we haven't. He left VisTec Monday afternoon sometime after five. Almost everyone else was gone, and no one remembers seeing him leave. The receptionist got a voice-mail message saying he wouldn't be in for a few days. That's it."

Wade frowned down at his desk. "Sounds like our boy all right—he's AWOL."

"I don't know. According to the people at VisTec, this isn't unusual. Dowling is one of their telecommunications specialists. He travels a lot, and often at very short notice. He also puts in a lot of overtime, so when he wants to take off, he just goes. They don't seem to have a problem with it."

"Where does he go?"

"Skiing. And Miss Lloyd was telling the truth about that. He goes all over. Panorama. Lake Louise. Nakiska. Sunshine. Even British Columbia and down into Montana." Evan sighed heavily. "We haven't been able to narrow it down any more than that. There's no record of his taking a plane or renting a car, but he could be using an alias. Someone suggested he might have met up with some of his skiing buddies and gone off with them, but no one has a name."

Of course they wouldn't. Orion didn't hire idiots. Dowling would have covered his tracks well.

"We'll find him," Evan insisted. "It'll just take a little time, that's all."

"Right." Wade wasn't convinced. Mark Dowling probably had some sort of backup plan. He'd know Orion's crowd was on to him. He'd find himself a nice little hiding spot and lie low for a while. That's certainly what Wade would do.

Evan spoke again. "I'll keep you informed, Commander."

"You do that." Wade remembered the original reason for his phone call. "Listen, Evan, you got any information on a car accident late Monday night? Fellow named Karl Leros was killed?"

There was silence for a moment. "Uh-huh. I've got the report right here. Why?"

Wade told him about Rigel's visit. "I'm just wondering if there's any sort of connection, that's all."

"Looks like an accident," Evan said after a moment. "His car slid off the road and rolled into the ditch. Leros wasn't wearing his seat belt. There's nothing at all suspicious about it."

"What was the man wearing?" Wade asked.

Another silence. "A green ski jacket."

So much for that theory. "Guess it's nothing," Wade grunted. "Let me know when you track down Dowling."

He hung up the phone and leaned back in his chair to consider the situation. The police hadn't found Mark, probably because he was in hiding. Sooner or later they'd track him down, but Wade would rather it was sooner than later.

It might be best if he had another chat with Cass Lloyd. She might have heard from Dowling. Or Dowling might be expecting Wade to keep in touch with Cass. He might be expecting Wade to keep her safe. From the sound of things, Mark was as fond of his cousin as she was of him.

He should touch base with her again, although Evan wouldn't much care for the idea. He could hardly object, though. Wade was just keeping a date. He thought of Cass's brightly clad figure standing in Mark's hall, telling him she was all scared out. She'd invited him to drop by her store today and give her another scare. It'd be rude to stand up the little lady.

He stroked two fingers across his mouth. He knew just how he was going to scare her, too, and he was going to enjoy doing it.

He gave his head a quick shake. Information, he reminded himself. He was going to see her again because he needed to find out something.

It had nothing to do with those mottled green-and-brown eyes, the odd way she had of making conversation or that tasty bottom lip of hers.

# 7

THAT WASN'T any good, either.

Cass frowned at the bridesmaid's dress she'd just designed and shook her head. It would look wonderful on the tall, skinny woman, but wouldn't do a thing for the one with the big hips. Honestly, it would be so much easier if the bride had friends with similar figures.

She set down her sketchbook and rubbed the back of her neck. It couldn't be more than six-thirty, but she felt as if it were midnight. Maybe she should leave this for tomorrow. She yawned and regretfully rejected the idea. There was simply too much to do. Mrs. Hammond's dress was still sitting on the far corner of the workbench, waiting to be basted together, she had three wedding parties to clothe and tomorrow was partially booked up with appointments. If this kept up, they were going to have to hire a seamstress to give her a hand.

She picked up her sketchbook, and sighed. It hadn't helped that she'd wasted so much time today trying to find Mark. No one at VisTec knew where he was. She'd tried a couple of his friends, then decided to give his mother a call. That had been a major mistake. Cass had done little since then except talk on the phone, repeating the same story over and over to concerned relatives.

She'd been answering the phone all day, and not one of the calls had been from Wade. That must mean she was right, that he'd figured out all the "too" things that made her unsuitable. She imagined his big, solid shape and felt a pang of regret. "Oh, stop it," she told herself crossly. Even if he had called, she wasn't impractical enough to see him again. Lydia might think it was silly to reject someone she liked, but Cass was positive it was a very realistic thing to do.

She doodled on the side of the page and thought about what Lydia had said. She was right about one thing—Cass did have an active social life. She dated lots of men, but she suspected they were attracted to her more because of her wardrobe than anything else. Men might want a practical woman, but they sure seemed happy to be with one who didn't look the part! Later on, after they realized her impracticality wasn't just skin-deep, they'd come up with a list of things they wanted to change about her—and half the time, that included her preoccupation with her appearance! It seemed to Cass that the things they liked about her were exactly the same things they didn't like about her. It was probably some practical-reality issue, but it was definitely beyond her understanding.

She absently sketched an off-the-shoulder design and studied it. She'd had only two serious relationships in her life. Both times, the men involved had seemed to care for her exactly the way she was. After the relationship moved into intimacy, though, the men had discovered a whole bunch of things about her that made her unsuitable. In both cases, it had hurt a great deal. Cass didn't want that to happen again.

She made a couple of adjustments to the bodice of her drawing. Perhaps she'd call that dentist she'd met last week. He'd asked her out, but she'd been booked up with Charlie. Now she wasn't, the dentist seemed nice, and she did have decent teeth. Also she hadn't been that attracted to him. Perhaps . . .

"Cassandra Lloyd?" asked a familiar, drawling voice.

Cass dropped her sketchbook and swiveled her chair around.

Wade stood exactly where he'd been standing last night—a large figure dressed in the same jeans and denim jacket.

"Hi, baby," he said.

"Hi," Cass breathed. She studied him with mouth-watering appreciation, while her heart skipped a beat, then picked up speed. He was just as masculine and attractive as she'd remembered. *You're not going to see him again*, she reminded herself. But she couldn't help doing it if he was in her store, could she?

"You about ready to go?" Wade asked.

Cass blinked at him. "Go?"

"Uh-huh." He frowned sternly across the room at her. "You shouldn't be here so late all alone anyway. Where's your coat?"

Cass was still trying to assimilate the fact that he was there, and that he seemed to think they were going somewhere. "It's, uh, in the closet but . . ."

He turned away. "I'll get it for you. You can drive that Camaro on over to your place. I'll follow. Then we'll find someplace to eat."

Eat? What on earth? Cass swiftly replayed as much of their conversation last night as she could remember. None of it had involved food in any shape or form.

Wade was already rummaging through the closet. "Which one of these fancy coats in here is yours?"

"The . . . uh . . ." She tried to recall which coat she'd worn today. "The brown-and-blue one. But I don't . . . I . . ."

He pulled out her coat. "This it?"

"Yes, but . . ."

He held it for her. "Don't just sit there staring at me, honey. Let's get on with it."

Cass actually started to rise. Then she realized what she was doing and sank back down. "I can't go anywhere. I've got all this work to do."

"You should have thought of that before you invited me over."

"*I* invited you?"

"Uh-huh." He grinned widely. "You asked me to come on over and give you a good scare."

Cass moistened her lips and made a valiant attempt to understand what he was talking about. Then she remembered the scene in Mark's front hall last night. She hadn't considered that an invitation, but apparently he did. "I didn't realize scaring included eating."

"Now you know." He shook her coat. "Come on."

Cass didn't move. Just looking at him brought back all the feelings she'd had last night. An evening in his company would only make that worse. The sensible thing to do would be to refuse. But how could she refuse an invitation she'd apparently issued herself? Besides, she didn't want to refuse. The idea of a few more hours in his company was tremendously appealing.

She crossed the room and slid her arms into the sleeves of her coat. What the heck. She could always be practical and realistic tomorrow.

WADE DIDN'T even bother reading the menu. "I'll have a steak, rare, but not too bloody, baked potato, no dressing on the salad. Bring me a beer now, and another one when you bring the food." He settled back into his chair and began to unobtrusively scan the room.

The waiter gave Cass a questioning look. "I'll have the chicken special," she said with rare decisiveness as she handed him back her menu. She had no idea what it was, but there was bound to be one. "And I'd like a glass of water, too, please."

"No ice in that," Wade added. He turned a suspiciously bland face in her direction. "Hard on your teeth."

"Oh," Cass murmured. Wow! She'd never thought of that, but it was probably true.

She settled back in her chair and covertly studied Wade. He was wearing a brown cable-knit sweater tonight, and it looked as good on him as she'd thought. She liked the way he sat—relaxed, yet alert and somehow very tough. And very, very sexy.

And far too practical for her. As she'd suspected, Wade was so good at life's details that it almost made her dizzy. He hadn't waffled about asking her for restaurant preferences, or even what she liked to eat. He'd just brought her to a place that served a wide variety of everything, in a medium price range. He'd had no problem getting a parking space near the front door, and he hadn't even needed the maître d' to seat them. He'd just looked over the room, picked a table off to one side with a good view of the fireplace and announced "We'll sit there."

Cass followed the direction of his gaze toward a new arrival being shown to a table across the room from them. "He's a policeman," she informed Wade.

Wade swiveled around to face her. "How's that?"

"The man who just came in." Cass watched him take his seat. "He has to be a policeman. They're the only ones I know who wear that color. Maybe that's why they're called plainclothes. That's the plainest color I've ever seen."

Wade bit back a chuckle and took another look. "Guess that is the color Evan had on last night." He turned back to her. "How about these other folks? You got any idea what they do for a living?"

"Some of them," Cass admitted. She glanced around. "Those four men over there are oil-company executives. They all have the same company pin on their lapels, their suits almost match and their ties are all extremely conservative. That's oilmen. And that man over there is a real-estate agent—they always have gold cuff links shaped like golf clubs. The fellow across from us is an accountant—they usually wear white shirts with brown stripes." She peered over her shoulder. "That man's an engineer—he's got one of those watches only an engineer can figure out. The man with the flamboyant tie is a salesman of some sort—probably cars."

Wade produced a slow, admiring smile. "You ever considered joining the navy? You'd be one hell of a good addition to a recon team."

Cass's entire body tingled at his praise. She gave him a delighted smile. "Thank you, but...uh...I don't look good in navy blue. You do, though. That uniform really suits you." She suddenly remembered that the only time she'd seen him in his uniform was when she'd read his image off his medallion. "I mean . . . uh . . . I imagine it would."

Wade's eyes narrowed suspiciously, but before he could ask questions, the waiter arrived with their drinks. Cass breathed a relieved sigh and reminded herself to be careful. There was no way a person like Wade would understand her inexplicable little talent.

As soon as the waiter left, Wade stretched forward and rested his forearms on the edge of the table. "Have you heard from that cousin of yours yet?"

"Mark?" Cass asked. "No, no, I haven't. I did try, though. VisTec doesn't know where he is. I asked a couple of his friends and they don't know. And then I decided to call his mother." She shook her head. "That was a mistake. Aunt Doreen called Mom and she called me and then both my sisters-in-law phoned, and Mark's sister, and a couple of other aunts...." She sighed. "My brother Tom was even going to fly out here. And my other brother, Rick, thinks I should move to a better location. I have no idea where he got that idea. It wasn't even my house that was broken into."

"Any of them know where Mark's at?"

Cass's gaze went to his hands, and she remembered how warm they'd felt holding her head last night. "No. I really didn't think they would. He...uh..." She forgot what she was saying and had to start over. "He doesn't keep in close touch with them."

"Any particular reason for that?" Wade asked.

Cass lifted her gaze from his hands to his face. "For what?"

For a long moment he stared into her eyes, and his own began to darken to the cobalt-blue shade she remembered from last night. Then he jerked his gaze away, and when he looked back, his eyes were their normal cool periwinkle blue, but there was a slight stain of color on his cheeks.

"Go on," he encouraged. "You were telling me why Mark doesn't keep in touch with his family."

"Oh...uh..." Cass was still flustered. She took a sip of her ice-less water to hide her confusion. "No, no, that's not what I meant. He's very fond of them, of course, but he doesn't phone them up every time he leaves town. Do you?"

Wade's lips curled into a slow smile. "I don't know Mark's family, honey. I'm hardly liable to call 'em up when I take a trip."

Cass flushed and stared down at the table. She wasn't making much sense, was she? Perhaps if she didn't look at him, she could do better. "I meant, uh, do you keep in touch with your family?"

"Don't have much of one. Just my brother, Morgan. I see him every so often, but I wouldn't say we keep in touch."

There were two of them like this? "Is Morgan in the navy, too?"

Wade shook his head. "Nope. He's in Montana. He took over the ranch after our father passed on."

Cass mentally pictured a Wade look-alike, complete with horse and cowboy hat. "Why didn't you?" she asked. She watched his wide hand wrap around the beer mug, then glanced up to see him squinting at her with obvious puzzlement. "Ranch," she explained. "Why didn't you ranch? You look the type."

Wade took a swig of beer and shook his head. "I might look it, but I'm not. Every now and then I get a hankering to see the place, but after a few days, I'm mighty grateful to leave." He leaned forward and lowered his voice. "Cattle aren't what you'd call mentally gifted creatures. And they never do what you tell 'em."

"*You* have that problem, too?" Cass exclaimed. She'd never been any use dealing with the livestock on her parents' farm. If the cattle wouldn't listen to him, it was no wonder they wouldn't listen to her. "Is that why you joined the navy? Because you didn't like cows?"

He chuckled and nodded. "That was part of it. My dad served in the navy during the war. I figured I'd give it a try. Joined up as soon as I finished school."

Cass considered that while the salad was served. "Did your mother make a fuss about your leaving home?" she asked after the waiter departed.

Wade picked up his fork. "Never really knew the woman. She passed on soon after I was born."

"Oh, dear." Cass felt terribly sorry for him. "That must have been hard for you—growing up without a mother."

He munched away, unconcerned. "I don't recall it being any big hardship. Just the way things were, that's all."

"Did you have aunts around, or other relatives who could . . ."

"Nope. My dad had a brother in Arizona, but we never saw much of him."

Cass drew a mental picture of this ranch of his, populated only by three men. "Did you have a housekeeper or something?"

"No need for one. Dad and Morgan and I took care of things."

And didn't do much else, Cass guessed. She wasn't good at the duties of a farm wife, but she knew how much her mother contributed to running the place. Every other farm wife she knew did exactly the same thing. Looking after a ranch alone was a lot of work. "Is your brother married?"

Wade shook his head. "Morgan is kept busy running the ranch. Doesn't have time to bother with that sort of thing."

Cass ignored the food in front of her and watched him eat. "So at Christmas there's just you and Morgan?"

Wade shrugged as if it didn't matter. "Don't generally make it back for that."

"You don't?" This was just getting worse and worse. "What do you do then?"

He lifted another forkful of tomatoes and lettuce to his mouth. "Depends where I am at the time."

Cass watched him chew. "What does Morgan do at Christmas?"

Wade swallowed. "I have no idea."

He didn't look as if it bothered him not to know, either.

Cass picked up her fork and speared a piece of lettuce. Morgan and Wade sounded really practical, all right, but she sure didn't think it sounded like any fun. They didn't even seem to care about one another. Look how lucky she was. She'd just been complaining about all her relatives calling her, but they did it because they cared. "I hope Morgan has a lot of friends," she muttered.

Wade paused with his fork halfway between the plate and his mouth. "You've never even met the man. Why would you care if he has a lot of friends?"

Cass rolled her eyes toward the ceiling. For someone who seemed so practical, he could be a little dense. "It sounds lonely," she explained. "At least you have all the men in the navy. It doesn't sound as though Morgan has anybody."

"Morgan manages fine." He chewed away as if he really believed that.

"Does he?" Cass had her doubts. As a matter of fact, she didn't think it sounded as if either of these two managed just fine. It didn't sound as if they managed at all.

She pushed pieces of her salad around on her plate and covertly studied Wade. Was it possible to be too practical? She could learn a lot from him, but perhaps there was something he could learn from her.

She abandoned her salad and rested back against the cushions of her chair. "So tell me," she invited, "what do you do all day? When you aren't out intimidating people, I mean."

"AND NOW I SORT OF wander between security and training," Wade concluded. He watched Cass eat a small piece of the chicken dish she'd ordered, admiring the dainty way she had of doing it. She was wearing one of her brightly colored outfits, her brown hair gleamed with golden streaks and her cheeks were slightly flushed. She was the best-looking woman in the room, and she was with him. It was a pretty nice feeling, all right.

He did a quick check on Evan's man, chuckling to himself as he recalled how easily Cass had picked him out. Wade had spotted him when he'd stopped by Cass's store, and he knew they'd been followed here. Tomorrow he'd probably catch hell from Evan, but he wasn't concerned about that now.

He turned his attention back to his own meal. He seemed to be getting the hang of dealing with women after all. Cassie was incredibly easy to be with, and incredibly easy to talk to. She seemed so interested in everything he said, and so absolutely fascinated by his life that he was encouraged to talk.

"What about fun?" she prompted. "What do you do for that?"

Fun? Fun wasn't a part of his life. Wade couldn't recall ever doing something because it might be fun. "We don't generally waste a lot of time on fun."

"Well, you must do something in your spare time." She stopped eating and blinked those remarkable eyes at him. "You do get spare time, don't you?"

Wade shook his head. His work totally occupied him, and when he wasn't doing that, he was either talking about it or sleeping. "Don't have a whole lot of 'spare' time, either. What do you do with yours?"

"Everything," she said immediately. "I've always got a few craft projects to work on, as well as the clothes I make for myself. I'm always redecorating. Or shopping. Oh, and I do the costumes for an amateur theater group. Then there's the opera...." She wrinkled her nose. "I don't really like opera, but I love the costumes. I spend a lot of time with Mark when he's in town. And I go out a fair amount."

Wade cut a piece of his steak and contemplated her answer while he ate it. Her world sounded so alien to him that it was almost as if she were from another planet—a place filled with bright colors and friends and family and lots of other things to do just because she enjoyed doing them.

Cass broke off a piece of her bun and spread a surprising amount of butter on it. "Don't they let you out very often?"

"Out?" Wade asked blankly.

"Of that military base." She ate the piece of bun, and flicked out her tongue to catch a crumb. "Is that why you don't do anything for fun? Because they make you stay there and work?"

Wade's entire body started to heat up. Watching her eat a bun was almost as stimulating as watching her suck on ice cubes. "It's a military base, not a prison. We can generally come and go as we please."

"Oh." She took another small bit of bun and began buttering it. "It's sort of hard to tell the difference. Of course, I've never actually been inside one, so I wouldn't really know."

Wade couldn't imagine that. "You've never been on a military base?"

"No." She picked up her fork and resumed eating. "I even forgot there was one in Calgary. When I saw your image in that uniform, I had no idea where to find you. It wasn't until I had to go to Sue Hammond's place that I thought of the military base."

"Saw my image?" Wade repeated. He wasn't quite sure what she meant by that, although her casual tone suggested he was supposed to know. "You mean Mark showed you a picture of me?"

"Mark?" Cass glanced up, winced, then bent her head and busied herself with her meal. "No. No, of course he didn't."

"Then who did?"

"No one." She concentrated firmly on her plate. "It's not important, Wade. Really."

Wade studied her for a moment. She was obviously uncomfortable. Why? Was it possible she was more involved in this than he'd thought? He set down his utensils, ready to demand that she tell him, then changed his mind and decided on a soft approach. "It's important to me, honey." He reached across the table, caught her wrist and gave it a gentle squeeze.

Cass stared down at his hand on her and chewed on her lower lip. "Oh, all right," she said. "It's probably better this way anyway." She set down her knife and fork and raised her chin so she was looking him right in the eye. "Sometimes I . . . I read impressions from things."

Wade hadn't expected that. He concentrated on keeping his expression as blank as possible. Was this some sort of women's intuition thing? Did other women think they could do that, or was it just her?

Cass went on explaining. "I just touch something and think about the owner, and then I get sort of a . . . a mental picture of him or her."

"Huh," Wade snorted. He studied her face. Her eyes were wide and serious and very, very honest.

"It doesn't always work." She looked down at the table and then up. "I think it might have something to do with how long the person has had it and if they really like it. I mean, I won't get anything from a stapler, but I would from—" she shrugged "—from something like your medallion." She flashed a tiny smile. "I found it in the parking lot after you'd gone. I touched it and got an impression of you in a navy blue uniform."

*That uniform really suits you,* she'd said. A cold shiver curled up Wade's spine. Was this sort of thing really possible? No, of course it wasn't.

Cass watched him for a moment, then swallowed and put her hand out for her purse. "I don't expect you to believe it, but that's what happened and now, I . . . uh . . . it's a little late . . ."

Wade's mind clicked with lightning speed. She really believed this nonsense—she didn't expect him to, and if he said the wrong thing, she'd be gone. "That's a real handy talent," he said. He cut another piece of meat and then glanced over at her.

She was staring at him with openmouthed astonishment. "You . . . you believe me?"

Wade shrugged. "You're telling it like you see it, aren't you?"

"Yes, but . . . I . . . uh . . ."

"Well, there you go then," he said noncommittally. He gestured toward her plate. "You going to finish eating?"

Her entire face lit up; the admiration in her eyes beamed hotter and stronger than ever. "You really aren't all that practical, are you?" she breathed. "I have never told anyone about that before, you know. I thought they'd laugh at me or something. People are always doing that."

Wade watched her eat. He didn't for one minute believe she had held his medallion and gotten an image of him, but she was a very observant person. She could have gotten a glimpse of him, put that together with the military look of his medallion and instinctively come to the right conclusion about him.

Actually, it didn't matter. What did matter was that Dowling wasn't involved. He hadn't mentioned Wade to her, and he didn't seem at all like the type to be involved with Orion. The black suede jacket, the attempted theft of his car and the burglary of his house must just be coincidence.

Which meant Wade had no reason at all to see Cassie again. She ate another piece of bun and smiled at him, and Wade felt the last remaining bit of tension leave his body. It had been a long time since he'd eaten with a woman, and it would probably be a long time until he did it again. No reason why he couldn't relax and enjoy the experience. Later he'd take her home, have one final taste of her and then put her out of his mind. This time, for good.

IT WAS almost midnight when Wade unlocked the door to her house, and escorted Cass inside. She took off her coat while he prowled around the place, doing what he called a little recon to make sure it was safe.

She smiled softly to herself as she hung up her coat. She'd never expected Wade to believe her about that medallion. Now she was glad she'd told him. A man who believed that couldn't be all that practical, could he? Besides, it sounded as if he needed her. After all, he had the drabbest life she'd ever heard of. All he seemed to do was work, work, work. Even during his time off he worked, either at the ranch with Morgan or taking extra courses. Yet he hadn't criticized her life-style at all. As a matter of fact, he seemed totally fascinated with her. This relationship just might have a chance.

She heard him moving down the front hall toward her, and felt a warm, impatient tingle in her body. She was definitely going to see him again. She wasn't going to sit around waiting for him to call, either. She'd ask him over here. She smiled hazily at that thought. Then she'd have him alone all evening. That sounded delicious.

He returned to the front hall, where she was still standing, and stopped a few feet away from her. "No burglars tonight," he reported.

"Thank you," she breathed. She took a step toward him. "And thank you for the lovely evening. I . . ."

His eyes narrowed into dark cobalt slits filled with intent. "It's not over yet, baby. You still have a good scare coming."

"I think it's my turn to scare you." She floated toward him, circled her arms around his neck and pulled his head down. Then she put her mouth over his bottom lip and sucked on it gently, while pressing herself as close as she could to him.

He groaned, deep in his throat. He backed her against the wall and held her there with the pressure of his body. His hands framed her face, and his mouth stroked over hers, back and forth, up and down, until she was breathless and trembling. His hands dropped from her face, but she kept her arms around him and nuzzled his neck. "Oh, Wade," she whispered. She pressed soft, light kisses against his neck, knowing that if he wanted this to turn into more, she wouldn't object.

For a moment he just stood there, then his arms went around to hold her to him, his hand stroked down her back and his body gave one, long, violent tremble. "I've got to get going, baby," he said in a low drawl. He released her, put a hand on her face and gazed into her eyes. "You take care. And remember to keep your head down, huh?"

Before Cass could say anything he was out the door. Cass blinked at it a few times, stunned by the abruptness of his departure and by his words. They sounded awfully final. Wasn't he planning on seeing her again?

She flew to the door and yanked it open. Wade was halfway across her front lawn, heading toward his car. "Wade?" she called after him.

He paused and glanced over his shoulder.

"Tomorrow?" Cass invited. "Do you want to come and have dinner here tomorrow?"

He just stood there, and she thought he would refuse. "I'm not much of a cook, but...uh...if you're not doing anything you could...uh..." She couldn't see anything more than his shape, but she knew he was looking at her. "About seven," she said.

Wade's voice drawled out from the shadows. "I'll be here."

Cass remained in the doorway until he'd driven off. Then she closed the door, leaned against it and sighed. That hot embrace hadn't scared her all that much, but she didn't think she could say the same for Wade.

She locked the door and wandered into the bedroom to get Herman's opinion.

# 8

WADE WORE a black look as he walked down the hall between Captain Blackwell's office and his own. He'd been in a meeting for two hours with Keith Blackwell, he'd done most of the talking, and he had very little recollection of what had transpired. That sort of thing simply did not happen to him! Christ, if that had been a life-threatening situation, he wouldn't have survived.

It was all Cass Lloyd's doing. He'd had no intention of seeing her again, and yet he'd agreed to go over to her place tonight. He knew what would happen, too. She'd sit there, eyeing him as if he were desert, and he'd end up in bed with her. He didn't think he'd hear any objections from her, either.

He hadn't considered going to bed with her at all, until she'd thrown herself at him. Now it appeared to be all he could think about. He'd been aching for her since he'd left her place, a low, throbbing ache that showed no signs of going away. When he woke up this morning he'd done a swift mental calculation to figure out how many hours he had to live through until he was with her again.

He wasn't so sure seeing her again was a good idea. He'd only spent a few hours in her company, and already he was thinking things he'd never thought before. In the company of men, he had never felt lonely, but she made him feel as if he'd been lonely for a long time. He'd been perfectly satisfied with his life before, but she made him feel he'd been missing something. He'd even considered getting himself a place of his own when he returned to Washington. That was ridiculous. He hadn't needed one before; it would just take a lot of time he didn't have. And yet for the first time the thought of spending the rest of his life in officers' quarters didn't hold a whole lot of appeal. If he spent the night with her, he just might find something else changing.

There was no reason for him not to be with her, though. He was even ninety-nine percent positive that Dowling wasn't the man who'd contacted him, and that he'd had nothing to do with the return of Wade's medallion. That black suede jacket could be nothing more than coincidence, as could the attempted car theft and the attack at Dowling's house. An amazing coincidence, maybe, but still possible.

His best plan might be to show up at Cassie's, and get her out of his system. He'd be able to do that, wouldn't he? He thought of the married men he knew. They seemed to function fairly normally, but they did tend to focus on unimportant details, like how long they were going to be away from the little woman, or how much she wasn't going to like being transferred, or how she didn't like the quarters that had been assigned to them. Maybe he'd be best to stay away from Cass.

He was still mulling it over when he pushed through the glass doors leading to his office, and saw a burly figure in the vestibule. Damn! He'd forgotten that he should be expecting a visit from Evan this morning, along with another lecture about conducting his own investigation. He was in no mood for it now. As a matter of fact, if Evan started in on him, he might just tell him so, too. "'Morning, Evan," he growled. "Come on in." He led the way into his office and motioned Evan into a chair before settling into his own. "You folks found Dowling yet?"

Evan frowned darkly. "No."

Wade leaned back in his chair and tugged on his lower lip. "I'm not so certain he's the one we should be looking for anyway."

"I am," Evan said in a cold, deadly voice.

Wade suddenly realized Evan looked a lot more tired and a lot older today. "What's happened?" he asked.

Evan sighed and rubbed a hand across his forehead. "About four o'clock this morning, a security guard interrupted two men who were breaking into the VisTec offices. That's where Dowling works."

Wade felt the weight of the world drop back on his shoulders. "And?"

"And Dowling's cubicle was trashed. No one else's. Just his."

Wade frowned down at his desk. Damn! He'd been so sure Dowling wasn't involved in this. Cassie would be real unhappy about it. Damn!

"Security guard took two bullets," Evan went on. "And guess what? They're a good match for the ones we dug out of Dowling's house!"

Wade spent a minute reviewing all that had happened: the phone call from a man saying he worked for Orion, and that he'd be wearing a black suede jacket; the attack on Mark Dowling's car; the return of Wade's medallion; the black suede jacket Cass had found in Mark's car; the break-in at Mark's house, and now his office. Plus Mark Dowling was nowhere to be found.

Evan spoke again, confirming his own conclusions. "Someone's after him. It could very well be Orion's men, or it could be someone else. Whatever it is, I want to know what the hell is going on. And my only clue is Dowling. I want the man found."

"You want me to look for him?" Wade guessed.

"No, I don't, thank you. My original concern about you still stands. I want to know what Miss Lloyd had to say for herself last night." He paused meaningfully. "When you were out conducting your own investigation."

"I wasn't—" Wade stopped. If he hadn't been investigating, what had he been doing? However, it was hard to classify the relaxed, enjoyable evening he'd had with Cass as investigating. Actually, it came more under the heading of "fun."

"So?" Evan prompted. "What? Has she heard from him?"

Wade shook his head. "She hasn't heard from him, she doesn't know where he is and she doesn't know how to find him." He paused, thinking. "There's something wrong with this, Evan. From the things Cassie's telling me, Dowling doesn't sound like the type to be involved with Orion."

"I'll ask when I find him." Evan pushed himself to a stand. "I think it's time I had a little chat with Miss Lloyd myself."

Wade didn't like that idea. He climbed to his feet. "You think that's necessary? She doesn't know a whole lot."

Evan gave him a long, level look. "You're sure of that? After all, she's a very attractive woman."

"What's that got to do with it?"

Evan shrugged almost apologetically. "It's just that you wouldn't be the first to be sidetracked by a pretty face."

CASS FINISHED tidying the coffee table and put Herman's cage back on it. She'd been carrying him around from room to room with her while she cleaned, so he could keep her company. "Now, don't mess up the place," she told him. "We're going to be having company."

Herman gave her a quizzical stare and raced around in his wheel.

Cass waved her dust cloth at him. "This is a very practical thing to be doing." She gave the hamster one last look and danced into the kitchen. She'd been up since six, cleaning the house, making sure everything was perfect for tonight and making the difficult decision about what to serve. She'd finally decided on steak. After all, she knew Wade liked it, and she knew how to cook it.

She eyed her kitchen table, beautifully set for two. No candles. Wade wasn't a candle sort of a man. She could just picture him sitting here, looking perfectly scrumptious. She missed him. Already she was counting the hours until he was going to be here, watching her with his warm cobalt eyes, talking to her in the deep drawl that got slower and deeper the longer they were together.

She'd never felt like this in her whole life. She felt so important, so necessary. Wade needed her to brighten up his drab excuse for a life. He wasn't as practical as he'd first appeared; he already knew a lot of her faults and hadn't made any comments. Best of all, she was certain that underneath that practical exterior, he was just seething with impracticality.

Of course, he was only going to be here for three more weeks. Cass slipped on her coat and shoved away that concern. Perhaps thinking about that was practical but she wasn't going to do it.

She was just about to leave, when the front doorbell rang. She took a quick look through the peephole. Two men. Two big men. Both wearing...gray! One she didn't recognize. The other was that Inspector McCleod fellow she'd met at Mark's place.

Cass sighed and glanced at her watch. She was going to be late again after all. Oh well, this time she'd remember to find out where these guys bought their clothes.

She put on her best smile and opened the door.

"THERE'S A Cassandra Lloyd here to see you, sir."

Wade stared at the telephone for a moment. Was he so far gone he was imagining things? "Who?"

"Cassandra Lloyd, sir."

Wade checked the time. It was just before noon. Evan had left his office two an half hours ago—plenty of time for him to have talked to Cassie. Wade wanted to know what had happened during that interview. He also wanted to prove to himself that he was not sidetracked by her.

Evan's comment had got him thinking. He had almost believed her story about that medallion, no matter how illogical it was. He'd also managed to convince himself that Dowling was the wrong man. Two very poor conclusions for someone who prided himself on his ability to think rationally and logically about a situation. It could be that Cass Lloyd herself was involved and Wade was too "sidetracked" to see it.

Now she was here. He was going to see her, and he was going to prove to himself that he could keep his head when she was around. "Send her on in," he instructed.

He hung up the phone and stuck his head out of his door to arrange to have her ushered in as soon as she arrived. Then he sat down behind his desk and waited.

As soon as she stepped through his office door he realized keeping cool when Cass was around wasn't all that easy. She paused for a moment, a petite figure in a short black skirt, a long mauve jacket and laced-up, high-heeled boots that reached her knees. The sunlight caught the gold streaks in her hair, and the entire room seemed somehow brighter. Wade could smell her perfume, almost feel her body against his. His own body responded at once, heating to that restless, impatient ache. The response annoyed him, and he immediately, and irrationally, transferred that annoyance to her.

He rose to his feet and gave her a curt nod. "Cass," he said with no expression at all.

She pushed the door closed behind her and stomped across the room toward him. She stopped in front of his desk and gave him a glare that could have detonated a nuclear missile. "You didn't believe me at all, did you?" she accused.

Wade studied her flushed face for a moment, then sat back down. He knew how to deal with this situation. Every so often some character who figured he had a bone to pick would come stomping in just like this. The best thing to do was to let the fellow rant for a while, then gently spell out the mistake he'd just made talking to Wade that way. After that, the fight would pretty much go out of him and it would be possible to have a rational discussion about the situation.

He motioned toward a chair. "Think you'd better sit down."

She looked at the chair and made a face. "No, thank you. I can't sit in chairs that shade of green. It makes me feel like a lawn ornament." She turned on him. "I don't want to sit anyway. I've been sitting for hours while that dreadful Inspector McCleod and another dreadful policeman asked me all kinds of ridiculous questions."

Wade raised an eyebrow. "That so?"

"Yes, that is so!" Her voice rose again. "I don't know why they asked me anything, because they already knew most of the answers. I couldn't figure out how they knew until they asked me about that black suede jacket I found in Mark's car." She looked accusingly at him. "You're the only one I told about that. You must have told the police."

Wade eyed her suspiciously. "Any particular reason I shouldn't have?"

"Well, it's not very nice!" Cass exclaimed. "People like you shouldn't take advantage of people like me. It's not our fault we're like this. We just are!"

Take advantage of her? What the hell was she talking about?

"It's all because of that stupid medallion of yours, isn't it? The police asked me about it again, you know. I told them Mark had nothing to do with finding it, and they just *looked* at each other! Then I said you'd clear it all up and they just *looked* at each other again! Then they told me they'd already spoken with you and you'd done nothing of the sort."

Wade didn't see the significance of that. He sat there, waiting.

"That's when I figured out what you'd been doing!" She actually had the gall to shake a finger at him. "Wade Brillings you should be ashamed of yourself! That is . . . despicable!"

Wade didn't care for the sound of that. He lifted one corner of his mouth in a snarl, which she ignored.

"Now the police think Mark did something! Mark! That is so ridiculous. What does this medallion have to do with anything? You are the one who lost it! It's a very nice medallion and everything, but people wouldn't go shooting other people because of it! Mark wouldn't shoot anyone anyway. He certainly wouldn't go shooting someone just so he could wreck his own office. If he wanted to wreck it, he could do it without shooting anybody."

Her confusion was so obvious and so genuine that Wade felt some sense of relief. He hadn't been wrong about her. She had no idea what was going on.

She pounded a fist on his desk. "You call them up, Wade! You call them up right now and tell them they are making a dreadful mistake. Mark did not find your medallion. It happened just the way I told you, whether you believe it or not! I know I told you he had something to do with it, but I only said that because I was *scared* of you. I thought it was practical, but of course it wasn't."

Wade opened his mouth to speak, but apparently it wasn't his turn. Cass went right on talking.

"This whole thing is all my fault. I should have known someone who didn't care what his brother did at Christmas wouldn't care about how I felt." She graced him with another glare. "But I liked you! You shouldn't do that to people who like you. After all, there can't be that many of us, considering the way you treat people."

For no logical reason whatsoever Wade began to feel as if he had done something he shouldn't have. "I didn't—"

Cass drew in a breath and then ranted on. "And you even kissed me! Wade! How could you make yourself do that!" Her face contorted into an expression of utter revulsion, and her entire body shuddered with it. "It's . . . disgusting!"

That did it! "Sit down, Cassie!" Wade ordered in his softest, most dangerous tone.

She astonished him by arguing about it. "I am *not* sitting. I—"

Wade half rose and raised his voice to a bellow. *"Sit down!"*

She took a look at his face, dropped into a chair and continued to stare at him angrily. He wanted to walk around the desk and give her a good hard shake. And then he wanted to haul her up against him and kiss her until she was dazed and whimpering and not looking as if she wanted to scrub down because he'd touched her.

He clenched his teeth. "Now, you listen here, little lady. I don't tolerate people walking into my office and yelling at me. You got something to say, you'll do it with a little respect."

"I—"

"Don't you interrupt me! I don't tolerate that, either." Her mouth fell open, and Wade kept on going. "I don't know what you're making such a fuss about. I didn't hold a gun to your head or twist your arm to get you to say anything. And if the police ask me questions, I've got to answer them."

Cass made a movement to speak; he lifted a warning finger, and she subsided. "I am not responsible for the police actions in this or any other country. If they suspect your cousin of something, that is their business. And if they want to know how you found me to return my medallion, I suggest you tell them. You might consider telling them the truth, since they're no more likely to believe this cockamamy story of yours than I am." He watched her reaction. She was still glowering at him, still just itching for a fight.

"As far as this kissing thing is concerned, you weren't acting real disgusted when I was doing it—unless that little whimpering noise you make is how you sound disgusted!"

Her eyelids flashed down; her bottom lip trembled slightly, and she caught it with her teeth. He could actually see all the fight go out of her. Good. Now they could have a rational discussion about this.

Or perhaps they couldn't. Cass bounded back to her feet. She wasn't glaring anymore. She was looking at him as if he were the lowest form of life in the universe.

She wasn't shouting, either. She was yelling at the top of her lungs. "Of course I wasn't disgusted! I'm not the one who should have been disgusted. I was doing it because I liked you! I was attracted to you! That is the only reason you should kiss somebody! If you don't know that, then you've got more of a reality problem than I do!"

She whirled around and stomped toward the door. When she reached it she turned around and gave him another glare. "Not only that, but you look absolutely ridiculous in that funny-colored stuff you're wearing! You looked much better in your navy blue uniform. I know because I saw it when I touched your medallion!"

She stormed out, giving his door a good hard slam on the way.

Wade lifted a hand and stroked his forehead slowly.

Apparently he hadn't gotten the hang of dealing with women after all.

"AND HE DIDN'T know what he'd done!" Cass concluded. She glared at the contents of her workbench, which looked exactly as she'd left it last night when he'd ordered her to go out with him. "Now Mark's in big trouble, I've got all this work to do and it is all his fault!"

"Oh, dear." Lydia gave her shoulder a sympathetic pat. "I feel partly responsible, as well. I was all in favor of your dating him. I should have given it more thought. After all, he is an American and he is in the navy."

"Exactly," Cass agreed, although she wasn't quite sure what that had to do with it. She gazed up hopefully at Lydia. "You believe me, don't you? About my image-reading ability?"

Lydia examined one of her fingernails. "I know you're a very observant person."

Cass could tell an evasion when she heard one, but she also could tell Lydia was doing her best not to hurt her feelings. "I don't suppose Mark called, did he?" she asked.

Lydia shook her head. "No."

Cass sighed and sat back in her chair. "What am I going to do? The police are looking for him. The police! He'll be ever so upset if gets arrested. What will they do to him?" She glanced up at Lydia's anxious face. "They won't . . . put him on a chain gang or something, will they?"

"Mark?" Lydia shook her head. "Good heavens no. It's all a dreadful misunderstanding, I'm sure of it. No one who has ever met Mark would ever suspect him of doing anything illegal. He'll clear it all up when he gets back."

Cass felt slightly cheered by the confident tone in Lydia's voice. "Maybe I should talk to a lawyer."

"There's no point—not yet." Lydia gave her shoulder another pat. "A lawyer can't do anything unless Mark is charged with something. I am positive that as soon as the police meet him, they will drop any ideas they have about charging him with anything. If there is any problem, Tom's sister's husband's cousin is one of the best lawyers in town. We can get him to take care of it."

Lydia's sensible approach was very comforting, but it also added to Cass's feelings of inadequacy. Did everybody in the world know how to deal with these things except her?

She switched on her sewing machine, wondering if she could concentrate on anything today except how incredibly stupid she was feeling. "I wish there were something I could do," she said glumly. "I got him into this mess."

"It's not your fault at all. It's that Brillings man!" Lydia exclaimed. "Really! Imagine someone treating you that way. It's . . . reprehensible." As she moved toward the front of the store, she added, "If he comes around here, I will give him a piece of my mind. He's a terrible, loathsome man and I would enjoy telling him so."

Cass actually giggled at the idea of Lydia telling Wade off. Her smile faded almost at once. Lydia would probably be better at doing it than Cass had been.

This whole thing had made her feel more reality challenged than ever. She'd actually thought Wade had impracticality potential, that he was interested in her because he was attracted to her, too. When she'd realized Wade had told the police every bit of information she'd recounted about Mark, she'd asked them if Wade was working with them. Inspector McCleod hadn't confirmed it, but he hadn't denied it, either. He and that other policeman had just exchanged a look and stared down at the floor.

It had been incredibly humiliating.

She had been absolutely furious and very hurt. She'd actually lost her temper, something she hadn't done for years. It had been a waste of time, though. Wade had just sat there with his "who cares" expression and then had given her a list of things he didn't tolerate! She shouldn't have gone to see him at all. It had just added to her humiliation. She was glad she'd yelled at him, though; he deserved it. She pictured him sitting behind his desk in that funny-colored green-and-brown stuff, and felt very close to tears. She blinked them back. She was not going to cry over him.

He hadn't been interested in her at all, he hadn't believed her story about the medallion, and if she had half a brain, she would have realized that a lot sooner. Thrilling kiss aside, all he'd really wanted was a whole bunch of dirt on her cousin. She'd given it to him, too, at least she assumed she had. Now a whole lot of practical people had taken her little bits of information about Mark and come to some totally impractical conclusion.

It was such a dreadful mess. Mark was in trouble because of her, she couldn't think of anything to do about it and the only good thing was that she'd hadn't let Wade seduce her. Actually, she couldn't really congratulate herself on that, either. She had been perfectly willing to sleep with him. He was the one who'd backed off.

For some reason, that made her feel somewhat better. At least he wasn't a total creep. And she was positive he had no idea how bad he'd made her feel.

She shook her head at her own impracticality. After all that had happened, she was still just as enamored with him as ever.

She had to be the most impractical person in the world!

EVAN WAS the one who filled him in.

Wade called him up about ten minutes after Cass left his office. He'd gone over his conversation with her a number of times, and he still couldn't figure out what Cass had been having a fit about. He knew it had something to do with him, and with Evan questioning her, but beyond that, he couldn't make out what he had done to set her off like that.

Evan sounded more worn and tired than he had earlier in the day. Half of the ski country was blanketed by a blizzard, which was slowing down the search for Dowling, the security guard wasn't making much progress, and the interview with Cass Lloyd hadn't helped their investigation.

"We didn't find out anything from her," Evan complained. "She went off onto some tangent about your medallion, another spiel about that thing in the parking lot, and then she got all wired up about our clothes."

That didn't sound like anything to get her upset. "She was just here to see me," Wade admitted after a moment. "She was all riled up, Evan. You got any idea why that would be?"

Evan was silent for a moment. "She figured out where we got our information about Dowling. We didn't tell her, but she put it together. She was . . . upset."

"I know she was upset! I want to know why!"

There was another silence, then a long sigh. "Women don't like to be used like that."

Wade rubbed the back of his neck with his free hand. "Used?"

"What you were doing," Evan said impatiently. "You were using her to get information about her cousin. She had quite a little thing for you, you know, and she was under the impression that you were personally interested in her." His voice hardened. "I told you not to go off conducting your own investigation! We might have gotten some information that way, but it was pretty unpleasant watching her make the connection between you and our reason for being there."

Evan sounded almost accusing, and Wade felt a little guilty, although there was certainly no cause for him to feel that way.

"You'd better stay away from Miss Lloyd," Evan advised. "She won't want anything more to do with you, and I can't say as I blame her. She doesn't know anything, and even if she did, I doubt very much that she'd share it with you."

Wade hung up the phone and leaned back in his chair. Used? Personally interested? What was all this? He'd gotten a lot of good information from men this very same way—having a beer with them, letting them talk. No one had stomped into his office and ripped into him because he'd done it and no one had ever accused him of using another person, either.

He got to his feet and prowled restlessly over to take a look out the window. The snow was white, the buildings a dull shade of off-white and the roads a drab gray. The whole scene reminded him of a colorless movie. It was depressing; the whole situation was depressing. He felt as if he'd done something questionable, and he didn't like it. For christsake, it wasn't his fault Dowling had contacted him, and it wasn't his fault Cassie had returned his medallion. It wasn't his fault she'd looked at him with that "come and get me" expression in her eyes. If she'd misinterpreted his motives, that was her problem. He hadn't done anything more than spend a few hours with her. She'd talked; he'd listened. And he hadn't kissed her to get information! The kiss hadn't told him anything, except that she tasted good. It certainly hadn't been disgusting! He wasn't the one who'd suggested they see each other again, and he wasn't the one who'd suggested they sleep together. His muscles clenched at the idea and he pushed it ruthlessly from his mind.

Actually, he was relieved this had happened. Now he didn't have to decide if he was going to see her again. Apparently the decision had been made for him, and it was the right decision. He had no talent whatsoever for dealing with women, he wasn't interested in getting involved with one and they just made a man feel bad about things that were not his fault. He was sick to death of thinking about Cassie, he was tired of feeling unable to control his own body and he was grateful that this little episode was over.

Now he was going to put her out of his mind.

THE LITTLE LADY wasn't going.

Wade sat in the officers' lounge with three other men and pretended to listen to the conversation. They were discussing a lecture he'd just given, one they appeared to have found fairly interesting. Wade was surprised at that. He had little recollection of it, but he was pretty sure it was his worst lecture ever. He'd lost his train of thought several times, he'd had difficulty answering the simplest of questions and at one point he'd started talking on an entirely different topic. No matter what he did, Cassie's accusing little face remained with him, distracting him. The restless ache in his body had become almost desperately painful and impossible to ignore.

He checked the time. Eighteen-hundred hours. If this whole thing hadn't blown up in his face, he'd be getting ready to go over to Cassie's about now. He could just imagine her moving around that tiny kitchen of hers, forgetting what she was doing while she chatted away to him, every now and then giving him one of those admiring glances of hers. His mind flashed an image of what she'd look like with nothing on, the ache in his body increased, and he gritted his teeth.

He would live through this. He'd been on survival-training courses, resistance-to-interrogation courses . . . and had encountered things in the line of duty that had been fairly unpleasant. Of course, he'd known that sooner or later all those things would end. The way his body ached for Cassie didn't feel close to ending. He had visions of himself going through every day like this, and mentally groaned. If he didn't find some way of stopping it, they'd have to order up a firing squad to put him out of his misery. And firing squads took one hell of a lot of paperwork!

He pushed himself abruptly to his feet. Nothing had changed since last night. Okay, she was in a snit, but she could darn well get over it. She was wrong anyway. If this whole thing was about his reasons for being with her, well, they weren't all because he wanted information. He didn't want any information now, and he still wanted her. Was that "personally interested"?

He mumbled something to his companions and strode out the door. Somehow little Miss Lloyd had gotten into his system. He had to do something to get her out.

# 9

"AT LEAST the house is clean," Cass told Herman.

He stopped running in his wheel long enough to look at her with total disinterest, then started again. Cass lay back on her white wicker sofa and listened to the squeak, squeak, squeak of Herman's wheel. It was driving her nuts, but at least it was a distraction.

She had spent the afternoon concentrating steadily on pretending Wade Brillings didn't exist. It was her way of handling people who upset her, and it usually worked. When Eddie Barker had told her she was too flighty and she'd given him back his ring, she'd coped by using her he-doesn't-exist method. When Joel McMaster had announced she was too untidy and she'd told him to move out, it had helped her again.

Naturally, it didn't work for Wade. Cass wandered into the kitchen, took one look at the still-set table and returned to the living room. She'd had such big plans for tonight. She sat down in a chair and imagined Wade sitting on her sofa. What would he have been wearing? Another sweater? Maybe navy blue this time. She tortured herself by picturing him in different colors and styles, and feeling worse and worse with each passing minute.

She was jerked back to reality by the sound of the doorbell ringing. It gave one long peal that was immediately followed by a fist banging against the door. A slow, knowing shiver tingled up Cass's spine. "Who do you suppose that is?" she asked Herman.

Herman stared at her.

"That's who I think it is, too," Cass agreed. She glanced at her watch. Seven o'clock. Surely even Wade would realize that the dinner invitation had been rescinded. Of course, she hadn't exactly said so, but . . .

The doorbell rang again, the fist pounded on the door again. Cass moved hesitantly to peer through the peephole, and her heart gave a giant leap. It was Wade, all right, and even in the distorted view of the peephole, he looked strong and yummy and incredibly irresistible. Cass rested her forehead against the door and groaned. She didn't want to have to face him again, but she didn't think she had a lot of choice. A locked door wouldn't stop Wade if he wanted to come in. She might as well open it. Then she'd tell him again what an utter creep he was, and that he should go away and never come back!

She took a quick peek in the hall mirror. She'd thrown on her jeans and a long, bright-pink shirt, so at least her clothes were okay. However, her hair was all over the place, her mascara was smeared down her cheeks and she looked pale and miserable. There wasn't much she could do about it now, though. If she didn't hurry, he'd break down her door or smash a window or come down her chimney. Darn the man! Oh well, it didn't matter a whole lot what she looked like, did it? She unlocked the door and opened it a tiny crack. "Go a—" she began.

She didn't even get to finish that two-word sentence. Wade gave the door a hard shove and pushed past her into the hallway. Cass took an instinctive step backward; Wade slammed the door closed, barring her from it with his body.

Cass stared miserably at his large, masculine figure. He had on his usual outfit—jeans, denim jacket and high boots. There was enough heat emanating from him to steam up her hall mirror, and she just wanted to burst into tears at the sight of him. "Go away," she said, but it didn't sound very forceful, and he completely ignored it.

Instead he studied her with narrow cobalt-blue eyes, then bent to take off his boots. "We're going to talk about this," he announced.

Cass swallowed hard. "There's no—"

"Never occurred to me I was doing something I shouldn't have been doing." He got his boots off and straightened. "I don't deal with a lot of women. Hard for me to know how they look at things."

Cass's spirits lifted slightly. Was this some sort of apology? "Oh," she said.

He shrugged off his jacket. "I don't have a lot of choice when it comes to the police. They ask me questions—I've got to answer them."

Maybe it wasn't an apology. What was he trying to tell her? That it wasn't his fault? That the police had forced him to talk. She couldn't imagine anyone forcing Wade to do anything he didn't want to do.

She opened her mouth to tell him so, and forgot what she'd planned to say. He had on a white shirt, with the sleeves rolled up to the elbows, and she could see the shadow of his chest hair underneath. For some reason she found that incredibly arousing. She sucked in her lower lip.

"You've got no cause for ripping into me like that," he went on in an aggravated tone. "You go around eyeing a man the way you eye me, you've got to expect some repercussions."

Now it was all her fault. Cass folded her arms protectively around herself and he went on.

"I'm not real clear on what 'personally interested' means, but if it means what I think it means, then I sure as hell am personally interested in you."

That sounded better. "Oh," Cass breathed. She'd had no idea her heart could beat this fast.

"I wasn't disgusted when I kissed you, either." He frowned sternly. "It didn't tell me one thing about your cousin, and I wasn't doing it because I wanted to find out anything! I was doing it for the normal reasons. You clear on that?"

Clear? She had absolutely no idea what he'd just said, but his eyes were gleaming at her, and her body was heating up and . . . "Well . . ." she began.

"Good." He took a step forward, clamped his hands around her face and held it up. His mouth came down on hers and urged her lips open, demanding, and getting, a response when they did. Then he released her and stepped back. "You got dinner started yet?"

Cass blinked at him, stunned and shaken from his kiss. "Not exactly, but . . ."

"I'll get working on it while you wash up." He put a hand on her cheek and stroked it with his thumb. "I didn't mean to get you all upset, honey," he said in a light, raspy drawl. He brushed his lips lightly over hers, then strode off into the kitchen.

Cass leaned back against the wall and took a few deep breaths. Then she wandered down the hall and peeked into the kitchen. Wade was busy pulling things out of the fridge. Cass watched him for a moment, then continued on to the bathroom and stared into the mirror. "How on earth do practical people do it?" she asked her reflection. "Do they have a reference book or something?" She giggled rather hysterically at the idea. If there was a reference book, there would have to be an entire chapter devoted to Wade Brillings. No, more like an entire volume.

Her face looked back at her with wide, dazed eyes and a mouth that trembled slightly. Cass touched a finger to it and ordered herself to think rationally. Wade was here. He was either sorry for what he'd done, or he didn't think he'd done anything—she wasn't sure which. He seemed to think everything was settled between them. Heavens, he probably thought they'd just had some sort of deep discussion. She giggled again at her reflection. Honestly, he actually made her feel like a competent human being.

She watched the smile fade from her face. Was Mr. Practical Reality out there in her kitchen personally interested in her, or was he once more using her interest in him to find out more about poor Mark, who hadn't done anything?

She washed her face and began repairing her makeup. She probably should tell him to go. She heard a pot bang onto the stove and sighed. That was a really dumb idea. Wade wasn't going to leave and she didn't want him to go anyway! Besides she hadn't eaten, and it sounded as if he could cook. Why shouldn't they eat together? She wouldn't say anything about Mark and . . .

No, that wasn't the case. She was going to say a lot about Mark and a lot about Wade's medallion, too. She was going to tell him over and over and over that he'd made a big mistake.

It sounded pretty practical, didn't it?

"AND THEN she had me make a dress that exactly matched her wallpaper," Cass concluded. "It was lovely on the wall, but a green flowered print on Mrs. Medcalf was not very attractive. It didn't really matter, though, because when she walked into the room, she entirely disappeared!"

Wade chuckled and set down his utensils. Cass glanced down at her own plate and realized, with some surprise, that she'd eaten everything. "That was really good," she told him. "Where did you learn to cook?"

"On the ranch." Wade got to his feet and took her plate and his over to the sink. "It's part of survival training, too, although we don't often get anything as appetizing as this." He grinned at her over his shoulder. "More likely something like that hamster of yours."

"Mark's," Cass murmured. "Herman belongs to Mark." She frowned as she saw Wade's shoulders stiffen. She'd mentioned Mark's name three times, and three times Wade had reacted this way. He'd also refused to talk about his medallion, the police or even the scene in his office. He was very practical about it—he just told her they weren't discussing it. End of subject.

Her frown faded as she studied his back. Normally, she didn't like the white shirt-blue jeans combination, but on him they looked marvelous. A vest would be nice—a brown leather one, maybe. She drew in a breath at the image. She'd never imagined herself with the "home on the range" kind of guy, but Wade was . . .

Totally out of the question. She gave her head a quick shake. Yes, he was very attractive, but just look at the way he cooked! He'd broiled the steaks, he'd produced a salad where all the ingredients were almost exactly the same size and he'd even made mashed potatoes without getting potatoes all over the kitchen.

Actually, making the meal had been a lot of fun with him around. She didn't even mind his ordering her about. What she did mind, and what was becoming very difficult to deal with, was the way he watched her. His lack of expression was totally gone, replaced with a hot, possessive look that made putting together a sentence almost impossible. It didn't take a lot of imagination to guess what was on his mind.

It was her fault, of course. She could not stop herself from watching him, and every time she did, her mind went off on a little trip about how nice it was that he had clean fingernails, or how incredibly sexy his mouth was, or even the way his hand moved when he was cutting his meat.

He poured the coffee he'd made, carried it over to the table and sat down. It was so easy and so natural that they could have been doing this for years.

She took a long breath and looked straight into his warm, cobalt-blue eyes. "I want to talk about Mark. I want to know what the police think he's done."

Wade shook his head. "It'll just get you all riled up again."

"I'm already riled up, whatever that means. Mark isn't just my cousin—he's my dearest friend. It's my fault he's in this mess and—"

"It has nothing to do with you."

"Yes, it does." For some reason Cass wanted to cry. She blinked rapidly. "I owe Mark so much. It was because of him that I got to come here. He's always, always taken care of me and he never tells me that I'm too impulsive or too moody or too...anything. Then I went and found your medallion and...and...now I'm sitting here with the man who's trying to have him arrested, just because he looks scrumptious in a white shirt and..." She shook her head. "It's not right."

Wade bent his head and massaged one of his temples. "Are all women like you?" he asked.

"No," Cass sniffed. "They're mostly a lot smarter, a little taller, and not many have naturally curly hair."

Wade thrust his tongue into his cheek. "Don't suppose your particular model comes with a manual?" She shook her head and he sighed, long and mournfully. "Figured as much. Okay, honey, I will tell you what I know. But don't you go ranting at me again, you hear?"

"OH MY!" Cass breathed. She stared at Wade's hard, tough face in total astonishment. He was even more incredible than she'd imagined. Sneaking around dark parking lots on secret rendezvous with men as tough as he was.... It was like something from a movie. "Are you . . . some sort of spy?"

Wade shook his head. "Nope. I've had a little experience with covert operations, that's all."

"Oh." Cass didn't see the difference, but it wasn't something she knew anything about. Neither did Mark. "And this Orion man—he steals guns from you people?"

"Not guns, no." He leaned back in his chair, and his eyes grew cold. "They steal things of a more experimental nature. Prototype weapons. Plans. They don't just steal from us, either. They're real open-minded about it. They'll steal from anybody and they'll sell to anybody."

"Well, Mark wouldn't do anything like that!" Cass said decisively. She was so relieved she was almost dizzy. Lydia had been right. This was all a dreadful misunderstanding, and as soon as Mark returned, he'd straighten everything out. "Mark doesn't know anything about weapons."

"He doesn't have to. He could just be acting as an intermediary—transporting things from one country to another or passing on bribe money."

Cass was appalled at the suggestion. "He wouldn't do that! He's just interested in computers and skiing. He wouldn't do anything bad! He's a nice person, Wade."

Wade didn't say anything.

"And he didn't have anything to do with your medallion. Really."

Wade picked up one of her hands and examined her nail polish. "It doesn't make a lot of difference. There was that incident in the parking lot, then at his house and then at his office. Something is happening with him."

Cass watched his finger stroke hers, and everything from her hair follicles to her toes tingled at his touch. "That's just a tidal wave of crime," she murmured. "They're always having those."

"Could be," he grunted. His mind obviously wasn't on the conversation. He turned her hand over and studied her palm.

"But you don't think so?"

"It's one hell of a coincidence if it is."

Cass pulled her hand away from him. "Then that's what it is. Wade, will you listen to me? I don't know who was supposed to meet you in that parking lot, but it certainly wasn't Mark!"

Wade's lips tightened. "It was someone who was going to be wearing a black suede jacket. You told me you found one in Mark's car."

"I know, but it isn't Mark's! It probably belongs to one of his friends who just happened to leave it there."

Wade raised an eyebrow. "In the middle of winter?"

"That's what you think Mark did, isn't it?"

Wade shook his head. "I figure he stashed it there to change into as soon as he knew the coast was clear. Keep me from identifying him before he was ready."

"But it isn't his," she said again. "I know it isn't. I touched it. I got an image off it. I . . ." She looked into his suddenly expressionless face and frowned. "You just won't believe I can do that, will you?"

Wade looked down at the table. "It doesn't matter much now. The police have got to find him and find out what's going on."

"But he won't *know* what's going on!" Cass pushed herself to her feet and paced across the kitchen. "You are looking for the wrong man."

"The police will find that out when they talk to Mark."

"But . . ."

Wade stood up. "There's no point in chewing this over any longer. Mark will be fine. If he's not involved, the police will find that out. If he is, well, he's doing the right thing now, and we'll take care of him."

"He doesn't need—"

"That's the end of it, Cassie. If you hear from Mark, contact the police. Otherwise stay away from his house, and don't concern yourself about it."

Right, Cass thought defiantly. They were all making a terrible mistake and she shouldn't concern herself about it! She didn't bother saying it, because Mr. In-Charge there wouldn't believe her. "What's your title again?" she asked.

"My what?"

"You know . . . Captain or Corporal or . . ."

"Commander," he said. "And it's a rank, not a title." He undid the top button on his shirt.

"It's certainly appropriate," Cass complained. She watched him undo another button and felt a quick burst of unease. "Wade, uh, why are you . . ." Her mouth went dry as he undid another button and then another. "Why are you taking off your shirt?"

His eyes glowed hot and dark. "I'm taking you to bed." He unfastened the last button and pulled open his shirt, revealing a massive chest with a mat of sandy-red hair. "Don't plan on doing a hell of a lot of sleeping, either."

His hot male scent swirled around as he held out a hand toward her. "Let's get on with it."

Cass actually started to obey, before she realized what she was doing. "No." She shook her head. "We can't do that. We have nothing in common, Wade. You are the most practical person in the universe and I'm the most impractical. A relationship between us would never, ever work."

"That doesn't have a whole lot to do with it—at least I don't see it." Wade leaned back against the fridge door, legs sprawled wide, and studied her. "Look, honey, ever since we met, you've been eyeing me as if I were a full-course meal and you'd been on half rations for a month."

Cass bent her head and stared at the white-and-gray tile of her kitchen floor, feeling her face warm to an almost unbearable temperature.

"I've been looking at you the same way," Wade said.

Cass glanced up at him. He was staring over her head with a puzzled expression. "I don't understand it," he said. "It never happened to me before. I've been fighting it and fighting it." His eyes focused on her. "But I'm not even close to winning."

Cass was incredibly touched by this revelation. "That doesn't mean we should sleep together," she said, more for her own benefit than his.

"Then what do you suggest we do about it?" Wade demanded. "I'm sick to death of feeling this way. I don't need some woman messing up my mind so bad I can't think of anything else."

Cass almost felt sorry for him. He had absolutely no idea how to deal with something as impractical as this, and from the expression on his face, she could tell he was suffering. Still . . .

He took a long breath. "If you don't have the same problem, honey, tell me now. Otherwise, let's get on with it." He stretched out a hand and pulled her up against him. His heat engulfed her, his hard, hot, aroused body throbbed against hers, making it difficult for her to think. He held her face so she would look right at him. "I'm on the base ten hours a day, five days a week. The rest of that time, I want to be with you. You don't need to worry about getting pregnant—I'll handle that. You don't need to worry that I'm using you to get information, because I'm not. I'm just trying to get past this, that's all." He brushed his lips across hers. "If you don't want to be sharing a bed with me right now, we'll wait until you do. But that's just wasting time, Cass. Sooner or later it's going to happen. We might as well get started and get this thing out of our systems once and for all."

Cass chewed on her bottom lip and found herself actually considering it. After all, she had been willing to do this before. But that was when she'd thought the relationship had some chance of working. This didn't. She rested her forehead against his bare chest and sighed. "Oh, Wade," she whispered. "What am I going to do with you?"

"Well, honey, it's been some time since my last experience, but it isn't the sort of thing a man forgets. First off, I want you to take off your clothes. I've been thinking about you naked ever since you jumped on that Camaro, and I'm going to have myself one hell of a good look. If you want to do the same, you go right ahead. Then we'll lie down on that bed of yours. The first few times, I think it best if we stick with the standard way of going about it. We'll try to take it slow, but I'm not making any promises, not the way I'm feeling right now. When we're finished, we'll take a little rest, and then we'll do it all over again." He lifted her chin with his finger. "After three weeks of doing that every time we've got the urge for it, we should have this thing licked."

Cass almost collapsed at his feet, more aroused than she'd ever been in her life. His bare chest was rough and muscled under her fingers; her mind was filled with erotic images of them together.

It was going to happen anyway. Cass was positive of it. If she told him to go, he'd go, but he'd be back. Why not get it over with? It shouldn't take him very long to get her out of his system, especially if they spent that much time together. He'd come up with a list of "too" things and then he'd be gone. Maybe he'd be out of her system, as well. "You're right," she murmured. "That is what we should do."

His entire body gained another ten degrees. He kissed her again, then released her, took her hand and led her down the hall to her bedroom. When they reached the door, he stopped and turned to face her. "Do you want to think about this some more?"

"No," Cass said firmly. "I don't want to think about it at all."

He sat down on the bed and took off his socks. "Go ahead. Take off your clothes." He pulled off his shirt and set it neatly on the back of a chair. "You can start with that shirt."

Cass hesitated, then unbuttoned her blouse and dropped it. Wade unfastened his belt buckle and began to lower his jeans. "Keep going," he encouraged. She slipped off her bra and let it drop, then undid her jeans and wriggled out of them, unembarrassed because she was so entranced with the body he was revealing. There wasn't one ounce of fat on the man—his thighs were as muscled as she'd expected, as were his arms and chest and even his neck.

When he got down to his white cotton briefs, Cass stopped thinking about anything else but him. She stood in the middle of the room, stared in dry-mouthed eagerness as he stripped them off, then reached out to caress his large male length. He hissed in a breath and eased her down onto the bed. Then he carefully and gently and far too slowly arranged her across it, parted her legs and studied every part of her with eyes so narrow and so filled with passion that Cass could hardly breathe. He touched her with an awed gentleness, then watched his hands as they stroked her body from her neck to her toes.

"You are put together real fine," he said in a raspy voice slightly above a whisper. "Real fine, baby."

She held up her arms for him; he reached for his shirt and pulled a foil package out of the pocket. Then he was lowering himself onto her, gathering her to him, pressing his head down into her throat and sliding his hard, hot length into her.

After that, it was far too fast. He drove himself into her with quick, determined thrusts, while growling encouragement into her ear. "That's right, honey. You're so soft, and so tight. That's good. Ah, Cassie, that's real good."

He reached down between their bodies and stroked her, and she heard herself gasping with breathless astonishment as her body arched in climax. She felt his muscles clench, heard his pleasure-filled groan. Then he collapsed onto her, crushing her under him, while he shuddered with release.

Cass turned her head to one side, took long, deep breaths and closed her eyes. After a few minutes Wade lifted his head and spoke. "You all right, honey?"

"Mmm," Cass murmured. She patted his back, feeling the ripple of muscles under his roughened skin. All right? She was . . . splendid.

He moved slightly, shifted his weight to his side and pressed his hand on her hip to keep them joined. "If this is how it always feels, I'd sure like to know why I haven't done more of it."

IT WAS RATHER as if he'd taken her prisoner.

Cass lay flat on her back. Wade was stretched out on his side, with one of his arms holding her down and one of his legs thrown over hers for good measure. This was how they were sleeping, he'd announced. "I want to hold on to you all night, baby, so quit squirming around, get yourself comfortable and stay put." Cass had giggled at that. It was amusing to be ordered to cuddle.

She closed her eyes. Wade simply radiated heat. It was good thing they were doing this in the wintertime. In the summer, she'd melt.

She winced at the thought and told herself not to think about it. By summer she would be over him. And by summer, this whole mess with Mark would be all cleared up. "Wade?" she whispered.

"Uh-huh."

"The police won't shoot Mark or anything, will they?"

"Nope."

"You're sure?"

"Uh-huh."

"He's the wrong man," she said for what felt like the billionth time. "I know. I really can do that. I really can read an image off of . . ."

His hand caressed up and down her arm. "Don't concern yourself about it."

"Right," Cass muttered. He was just like every practical man she'd ever met. The police told her not to worry about anything—they would handle it. Lydia was the same way. So was Wade. They all acted as if she were some ditz with nothing useful to offer the world. Usually they were right, but in this case, they were wrong. "That's fine for you," she grumbled. "You don't even concern yourself with what your brother does for Christmas."

"He goes to the neighbors'."

Cass turned her head and peered into his face. How could anyone look so tough with his eyes closed? "What?"

"Morgan," Wade explained without opening his eyes. "He goes to the neighbors' for Christmas. Folks by the name of Jonston."

Cass squirmed over onto her side. "I thought you said you didn't know what he did."

"I didn't. I called him up this afternoon and asked." Cass's throat choked up. "You did?"

"Yup. Poor old Morgan thought I'd lost my mind. Good talking to him, though." He pushed her back into position. "Quit wiggling around and—" He stopped talking as she slipped down from under his arm, pressed her lips to his chest, then began kissing her way down.

She felt his muscles quiver under her touch, and fondled him to almost immediate hardness.

"You trying to tell me something here?" he guessed.

Cass drew her tongue across his abdomen, put a hand on his firm buttocks to hold him to her and took a few long, gentle sucks all the way up his length. She heard his breathing change, heard him growl deep in his chest and returned to her original position beside him. His eyes were wide open now, she noted. She closed hers. "Don't concern yourself with it," she advised.

From his reaction, she gathered that he didn't think much of that advice, either.

# 10

"I AM GOING to be early for work," Cass announced as she studied her reflection in the full-length mirror. "Really, really early. Do you always get up at five-thirty?"

Wade pulled on a sock. "Nope. By now, I've usually put in a good two hours." Her eyes widened and he grinned. "Might be a slight exaggeration. You didn't have to get up, you know."

"You woke me up," Cass accused, but the look she tossed his way suggested she wasn't complaining. She slipped off her purple shirt and threw it onto the bed, leaving her wearing a black skirt, a lacy green bra and nothing else.

"If you don't get some clothes on, I might wake you up some more," Wade warned as he watched her stare into the closet. He considered doing it, then decided, regretfully, that he didn't have either the time or the stamina.

Cass slipped him a smoldering look. "That so?" she muttered in a deep imitation of his voice.

Wade tried to appear stern, but he couldn't stop himself from grinning. Not many people had the nerve to make fun of him, but she did it with such a cheerful, flirty manner that all he could do was chuckle. He glanced at the pile of clothes on the bed beside him. "Why did you take off that shirt? It looked fine to me."

"I'm not in a mauve mood," Cass informed him. "Maybe I'm in a pink mood. No . . . red?"

Wade kept watching her. "Do all women spend this much time deciding what to wear?"

"No," she murmured. "I think I'm more indecisive than most."

"You just go on doing it," Wade advised. "As a matter of fact, any time you feel like taking off your clothes, you go right ahead. Just make sure I'm around to watch."

For a moment Cass seemed totally taken by surprise. Then she gave him one of her delighted smiles and turned back to the closet. Women liked hearing that sort of thing, Wade noted. He'd better remember that in case she ever got pissed off with him again.

He pulled on his other sock. Why in hell hadn't he done this before? He liked everything about it. He enjoyed waking up with her curled up beside him. He enjoyed waking her up, and he enjoyed the way she looked at him while he did it, blinking trustingly at him with those amazing eyes of hers. Camouflage eyes that didn't camouflage anything. This morning she was looking at him as if he'd just wrestled two or three grizzlies with both hands tied behind his back. Kind of made him feel as if he could do it, too.

He liked that feeling. He liked seeing how she got on with her day, listening to her vague little mutterings, watching her change her clothes two or three dozen times. And most of all, he liked knowing that tomorrow morning he was going to be here again.

He regretfully pushed himself to his feet. "I've got to get going, honey. What time will you be done tonight?"

Cass chose a pale-gray sweater with unusual, multicolored patches of pink and white and pulled it over her head. "I'm not sure," she said, her voice muffled by the sweater. She tugged it down and fluffed out her hair with both hands. "There's a key in the mailbox. You can just—"

"You leave a house key in your mailbox?"

"I have to," she explained. "I keep forgetting mine, or else I lose it in my purse." She glanced expectantly over her shoulder at him.

"Makes sense," Wade said immediately. It did, too, in a rather illogical sort of way. Darned if he wasn't getting the hang of the way her mind worked. And he was also getting the hang of those wary little looks she kept giving him. He interpreted them as meaning that he'd better watch what he said. Probably some woman thing he didn't understand, like how a person could be in a mauve mood. He was going to have to ask her to explain those looks to him, but he wasn't going to do it now. There was a time for discussions like that, and Wade figured the best time was right after he made love to her, or just before he was going to. That way, if she got upset, he had some ammunition at hand to calm her down.

At the moment, it appeared agreeing with her was the right thing to do. She gave him one of her "you are the greatest man in the universe" looks and his heart swelled. "I'll see you tonight," he said gruffly, and started for the door.

He heard a quick rush of movement and turned around, just in time for her to hurl herself into his arms.

"You're supposed to give me a goodbye kiss," she scolded. She reached up on tiptoe to press her soft lips against his cheek. "Like that." She moved away.

Wade grabbed her arm and pulled her back to him. "Nope," he announced. "I think it's like this." He took her head between his hands and touched his tongue to her bottom lip. She quivered against him, and he nibbled and sucked at her mouth until she was making those little whimpering noises he was becoming addicted to hearing. When he stopped, she slowly raised her eyelids to blink hazily up at him and Wade smiled with satisfaction. That was the look he wanted to carry with him all day.

THE LOOK he didn't want to carry with him was the one he saw on Evan McCleod's face.

He caught sight of Evan as soon as he stepped out of Cassie's front door. It was still dark, but Wade had no problem making out Evan's bulky shape, leaning against the passenger door of his four-wheel-drive. Wade took the key from Cassie's mailbox and hoped Evan was there to tell him they'd found Dowling, and that he'd turned out to be the wrong man.

However, from Evan's grim expression, he didn't think that was what was going to happen.

"You're driving me to work," Evan growled as Wade drew near.

"Fine with me." Wade unlocked the passenger door of his car. "You folks found Dowling yet?"

"No." Evan climbed in and slammed the door.

Wade winced at Evan's tone and rounded the car to get in behind the steering wheel. The leather upholstery was cold and hard under him, his breath was clearly visible in the frigid winter air, but as he started his car, Wade figured the coldest thing around was the look Evan gave him. "Something on your mind?" he asked as he drove away from the curb.

"Sure is," Evan grunted.

Wade took a quick sideways look at him, and immediately regretted it. Lord, he was tired of being chewed out by this man. "Go ahead," he invited. "Say your piece and get it over with."

"I intend to." Evan spoke with low, hard determination. "I have asked you several times to stop running your own investigation into this Orion business. Now, I know we're having a little difficulty locating Dowling, but we will. We don't need you, we don't want you involved. And if I have to make a few phone calls to keep you away from Miss Lloyd, I'm going to do it."

Wade pulled onto the main road that led to the downtown area and checked a lane change. "You go right ahead and give it a try if you've a mind to do it." He glanced again at Evan's features. "I'm telling you right now, though, that it won't do a hell of lot of good. How I spend my free time is pretty much my own business."

"It isn't in this case," Evan retorted. "She is not involved, at least not intentionally, and if Dowling contacts her, we'll know one way or the other. You don't have to . . . seduce her to—"

"I didn't seduce her!"

"You spent the night at her house! You going to tell me you were teaching her self-defense techniques?"

Wade glared at him. "I'm not going to tell you anything. My personal life isn't any concern of yours." He turned his gaze back to the road. He didn't often have a personal life, and now that he did, the police wanted to know all about it. Must have something to do with their being Canadian.

Evan leaned back against the seat and sighed. "It's not just your personal life. It's Miss Lloyd's, as well."

"I can handle her."

"Yeah, well, that's not exactly what I meant." Evan paused and softened his tone just a little. "She's a rather vulnerable woman, with a very trusting nature. You are going to hurt her very badly by leading her on like this, just so you can get information out of her. Now, maybe you don't give a damn, but I do. It's not right. I feel extremely responsible for letting it go this far. I don't like it, and if you won't put a stop to it, I will, even if means talking to the lady myself."

Wade took the downtown exit and stopped at a red light. He shifted to face Evan and looked him straight in the eye. "Cassie knows why I'm with her. I've been real up-front about it. And it's not because I'm interested in what she has to say about her cousin!" Evan didn't appear convinced and Wade tightened his lips. "Damn it, man, the woman got into my system somehow. I'm just trying to get her out, that's all."

Evan eyed him with a hard, searching cleverness. Then he nodded and settled back in his seat. "Why didn't you say so before?" he grumbled. "I hate having conversations like this."

The light changed. Wade drove carefully through the heavy early-morning traffic and felt more kindly disposed to Evan. After all, the man was just watching out for Cassie's well-being. You couldn't fault him for that.

Evan chuckled wryly. "It's not going to work, pal."

Wade kept his gaze on the car in front of him. "How's that?"

"Once a woman is in your system, you pretty much can't do without her. She's there to stay."

Wade glowered across the car. Evan was grinning from ear to ear, obviously getting far too much pleasure out of this. "There has to be something I can do about it."

"There is." Evan raised an eyebrow. "You make darn sure she feels the same about you, you invite me to the wedding and you name the twins Evan and Evlyne."

He was still chuckling when he got out of the car.

CASS STOOD at the front of the store window and studied the gray sedan outside. She knew very well the men inside it were policemen. As soon as this was over, she was going to go down to police headquarters and offer to help them buy all these plainclothes people new plain clothes.

She frowned at them. They'd been outside her house this morning, and they'd followed her here. They thought she was going to lead them to Mark, didn't they? Well, they were wrong. She had no idea how to find him.

"Is something the matter?" Lydia asked.

Cass hesitated, then decided not to tell Lydia about the police. She just might march out there and tell them off, and although it might be fun to watch, it also might get Lydia into a lot of trouble. She turned around and smiled at her. "No. Everything is fine."

Lydia studied her intently. "You seem a lot more cheerful today."

Of course she did. She'd just spent the night with Wade, a fact she hadn't shared with Lydia. She was sure Lydia would not approve and she didn't want to hear her objections. She knew what she was doing.

She wasn't sure Wade did, though. She'd expected him to start this morning with some criticism of her. Instead, he seemed to like everything about her. It could take him all of three weeks to find her flaws.

"Have you heard from Mark?" Lydia asked.

"No," Cass admitted. "I keep calling his house, but there's no answer. I have also talked to every single person at VisTec. They are really worried about him. I just hope the police don't contact Aunt Doreen. She will have another fit!" She turned toward the workroom. "I'd better get busy. I've got a lot of catching up to do."

"Don't worry too much about it," Lydia told her. "I've contacted Mrs. Lawrence. She'll be in next week to give you a hand with the sewing. You've got far too much on your mind with all this police business."

Cass gave her a grateful hug. "Thank you. I'll concentrate on bridesmaids dresses."

"All right." Lydia wandered over to check the till. "Oh, listen, darling, Tom and I talked it over, and we don't think you should be driving around in that car of Mark's."

"You don't?"

"No." Lydia's brow furrowed. "Tom agrees with me that Mark would never do anything illegal. It's you we're worried about."

"I'm fine," Cass assured her.

"I'm sure you are," Lydia said with no confidence at all. "The thing is, something does seem to be happening and it does seem to have something to do with Mark. It's probably utterly ridiculous, of course, but we'd feel better if you weren't driving around in his car. Tom took our old Pontiac in to the service station on the corner to be checked out. It's not in the best shape, but we feel it would be better if you were driving it, instead of Mark's car. You just leave the Camaro at the service station. They'll take care of it until Mark gets back."

"I can't do that," Cass objected. "It's not necessary and—"

"Please, Cass. I know it's probably silly, but we are concerned."

Cass saw the determined set of Lydia's jaw and sighed. "Oh, all right," she agreed ungraciously. She walked to the back of the store and sat down at her sewing table. Now Tom and Lydia thought she needed to be taken care of. Honestly, the entire world seemed populated by people who were more practical than she was, and they insisted on letting her know they felt that way.

The whole situation was so ridiculous! That black suede jacket had nothing to do with Mark. It belonged to one of his friends, that's all. If she could find the owner, surely the police would listen to him and realize that they were making a big mistake.

She picked up a pencil and opened a sketchbook. Let's see, what had that black-suede-jacket owner looked like? She made a couple of preliminary sketches and frowned at them. They weren't quite right. She tried a few more times, then gave up. The image had faded from her mind, much like words to a song. The only way to refresh it was to touch that jacket again.

Unfortunately, that wasn't an option. The jacket was at Mark's, the police had told her not to go there and they were following her. If she drove over to Mark's place, they would stop her and ask all sorts of questions, and no matter what she said she'd probably end up making it look as if Mark had done something else!

AT THREE O'CLOCK, Wade phoned. Lydia was at the front with a customer, so Cass picked up the phone when it rang and answered absently, "Creative Elegance."

"Brillings," he barked back at her, and for a minute she wasn't sure who it was.

"Wade?"

"Uh-huh."

"Most people say hello," she murmured. Just hearing his voice on the phone got her all worked up. She pictured him sitting behind his desk, and became even more aroused. "What are you wearing?"

He chuckled. "Not a stitch, honey," and that image turned her brain to mush. "You're a little low on food," he told her. "I'm picking up some, so don't concern yourself about it."

"Oh," she said. He could think about food? How immensely practical. "Okay."

"You want anything in particular?"

Him with cheese sauce? Cass blushed at the idea and tried to remember what food she had in the house. "I . . . uh . . . can't think of anything."

"Here's what I got." He read off a long list of items, including milk and eggs and bacon and apple sauce, and she was so taken with the thought of him sitting naked in his office, making up a grocery list, that she could hardly pay attention. "That sounds like everything," she said when he finished. It did, too. Every single thing in the grocery store.

"Okay." He hung up without even saying goodbye.

Cass replaced the receiver and giggled. Wade Brillings in a grocery store would be something to see. He'd probably attack it in some straightforward logical manner; he wouldn't lose his list and he'd get everything he'd gone in to get.

She made a face. What on earth was the matter with her? The more practical he got, the more she liked him. She was going to have to try to be more realistic about his flaws.

She really wished he'd hurry up and get some.

IT WASN'T until she lost the police that Cass thought about going to Mark's house.

She hadn't lost them on purpose. She'd noticed that they were behind her when she parked the Camaro inside the service station Lydia had directed her to, but she hadn't given them much thought when she left. She'd been too busy concentrating on how incompetent this all made her feel. Tom had everything arranged, so all she had to do was hand over the keys to the Camaro, and climb into the Pontiac. It had even been kept inside the garage, so it was all warmed up for her. A nice gesture, but all these people made her feel so incredibly useless.

She drove out the far side of the garage, then onto the main thoroughfare, and suddenly remembered the police. There were too many cars and it was getting dark, so she couldn't tell if they were behind her or not. She turned onto a side street and waited, but after a few minutes there was still no sign of them. It must have confused them when she changed cars. Oh well, they'd probably just go to her house, and she could meet them there.

She started toward home, then changed her mind. This was her opportunity. She could go to Mark's, get a quick reading off that jacket and make a sketch. Then she could take it around to his friends and see if they knew who the person was.

She drove past Mark's house, and around into the alley behind, feeling more than a little triumphant. She must be catching "practical" from Wade, because she'd realized that if the police were looking for Mark and following her, then they were probably also watching his house.

She parked the car behind the house and climbed out. It was just getting dark, the backyard looked creepy in the dim light and his bungalow seemed more sinister than it had the other day. She took a long breath and gave herself a quick pep talk. There was no one else here. There was no reason for her to be nervous.

She slipped through the back gate and used her key to unlock the back door. The place appeared exactly as she'd left it two nights ago. Cass didn't switch on any lights—she knew her way around and she didn't want the police barging in to ask questions.

She stopped when she reached the front hallway and smiled, remembering Wade standing in front of this door, glowering at her. She pawed through the closet, found the jacket and closed her eyes. At first there was nothing. Then there was a brief, faded flash of an image, and a dull, cold sensation that made her skin crawl.

Then the front door started to open.

Cass heard it first—the faint click of the door handle turning. She dropped her hand from the jacket and opened her eyes as the door opened just slightly. Terrified, she turned to run in the other direction, and saw the slight movement of a shadowy figure in the hall. She screamed, grabbed the lamp on the hall table and hurled it as the shadow shouted one word.

"Police!"

EVAN WAS wrong about this.

Wade parked his car in front of Cass's house and climbed out. The lights were off and the place was dark. He must have arrived before her. That wasn't surprising—he'd hustled off the base without even bothering to change because he'd been eager to be with her again. He pulled his duffel bag out of the car, along with the bags of groceries he'd picked up on the way here, and shook his head at how much pleasure he was getting out of doing things like this. It was just because it was different, that's all. Sooner or later he'd get tired of it. Sooner or later he'd want to return to the blank impersonality of the officers' quarters, he'd want to be totally immersed in his work instead of having Cass creeping around the corners of his mind and he'd stop wanting to sleep with her.

He was probably getting over her already. Oh, he'd still found himself thinking about her today, but it hadn't been anything like that horrible discomfort he'd experienced yesterday. He wasn't fighting it anymore, either—any time she crossed his mind, he just let it happen, and then he could get on with his work. A few more days of being around her constantly should pretty much put a stop to that, too.

He strode up to the door and used the key he'd taken from her mailbox to unlock it. He was going to have to speak to Cass about that. Actually, there were a few rules he should be making—like how late she could work all on her lonesome and how she wasn't allowed into parking lots alone after dark. She'd follow them, too. He'd see to that.

He took off his things and carried the groceries into the kitchen. He hadn't heard from Evan since this morning, which meant they still hadn't scared up Dowling. Damn! He wanted the man found, he wanted the matter settled and he wanted it done while he was in town. Cass was going to be mighty upset if she was wrong about her cousin. He wanted to be here when that happened.

He wandered around the house, enjoying the profusion of color everywhere. It was bright and cheerful, and totally different from anything he was used to. That was partly why he was enjoying this, he rationalized. He hadn't had a home to go to since he'd left the ranch. It was kind of a nice sensation. He stopped in the living room and watched Herman race around in his wheel. A pet rodent, for christsake. Darned if he wasn't starting to be fascinated by that creature himself.

He went on down to the bedroom, wondering what Cassie had finally decided to wear today. It wasn't what she'd had on when he'd left, because that sweater, along with a good dozen other items, were strewn across the bed. There were four pairs of shoes dropped helter-skelter on the floor, and bottles of makeup and perfume on the dresser. It looked as if twelve women had gotten dressed here this morning, instead of one. Wade tidied up after her, shaking his head. She certainly was an impractical person, wasn't she? He kind of liked it, though. Actually, he liked goddamn near everything about the woman.

"Make darn sure she feels the same way," Evan had said. Wade wondered if Cass liked as many things about him as he liked about her, then decided he already knew the answer. Her eyes told him exactly what she was thinking. Of course, before he left that look would be gone, because he'd be out of her system, just as she'd be out of his. He'd go back to his life and she'd be looking at someone else like that.

Lord, he hated that idea. He tortured himself with it for moment, then shoved it aside. It'd be best if he didn't go around thinking about the future right now. It would take care of itself.

A car pulled into the back parking space. Wade strode down the hall and reached the door just as Cass entered. She stood there, an endearing figure in a white coat with a large fur collar fluffed around her face and high-heeled boots. There was an air of suppressed excitement about her, although her eyes appeared just a bit wary.

"Oh, hi," she said.

"Something wrong?" Wade asked.

She peered into his face, then produced a slight, tentative smile. "Wrong?"

Wade's throat went dry. Suddenly he wanted to ask her something else, but he wasn't sure how to phrase it. "Didn't sound like that Camaro of Mark's," he said, instead.

"It isn't." She bent to take off her boots. "Tom and Lydia made me take their car. They thought it would be safer."

Wade gave himself a mental kick. He should have thought of that himself. "Good idea," he approved. He studied her face again. "You okay, honey? You look a mite pale."

"My blush probably wore off," she murmured mysteriously. "How...uh...long have you been here?"

"Just arrived."

"Oh." She swallowed hard and started working on that lower lip. Then she sighed with what appeared to be relief and studied him up and down, and her eyes gleamed with admiration. "Those clothes do suit you, you know. I shouldn't have said they didn't."

Wade was ridiculously pleased by her reaction. He released a growl, scooped her up and tossed her over his shoulder. "I look better without 'em," he told her as he marched down the hall.

# 11

HOW COULD anyone spend an hour doing her finger-nails?

Wade sprawled on the sofa in Cass's living room, reading the paper and watching her fuss with her nails. She was sitting crossed-legged on the floor, with an astonishing array of items scattered around her that apparently were needed for this fingernail ritual. She had on a greenish outfit tonight, although he didn't think green was the right name for the color. The pants had wide, full legs that swirled when she walked, and the top was very long and had a brilliant multicolored peacock climbing up the back and arms. Lounging pajamas, she'd called them, and she didn't wear anything at all underneath them.

He watched her spread polish on an already colored nail, then tried to focus his attention on the newspaper. This was turning out to be a real pleasant way to spend an evening: cooking dinner with her drifting around the kitchen, waving spoons and chatting and forgetting entirely what she was supposed to be about; eating with her and talking about everything that had nothing to do with work; planning what they were going to do tomorrow. It wasn't as exciting as rapelling out of a helicopter, or as mentally challenging as designing security procedures for a military base, but there was something about it that he was enjoying a whole lot.

He read another paragraph in the newspaper, then looked back at her. They'd spent a good hour in the bedroom when she got home, and he was in the mood for carrying her back there again. He just couldn't seem to get enough of her—as soon as they finished, he'd start wondering how soon they could start all over again. He must be making up for lost time here. If they kept this up, he'd have to be taken back to the States on a stretcher.

He scowled at the idea of leaving and pushed the concern away. He had plenty of time to get this out of his system before he went. Unless it took her three weeks to do her nails. "You've been at that for at least an hour," he complained.

Cass examined a hand. "It takes that long. First you put on the base coat, then you put on two coats of polish, then you put on the top coat, and finally the drying coat."

Wade raised an eyebrow. "Why do you do it?"

She bit down on her lip. "Because I'm too preoccupied with my appearance. It's one of my impracticalities." She glanced expectantly at him.

Wade mentally groaned. Getting along with a woman was a lot like landing an F-15 on an aircraft carrier on a moonless night—not a lot around to give a man his bearings. "I'm pretty preoccupied with it, too," he replied.

Cass blinked rapidly, then looked away. "You probably don't spend a lot of time studying my hands."

Not a whole lot when she was wearing no bra and a shimmery shirt like that. "Can't take my eyes off 'em," Wade lied.

For a moment she just stared at him. Then she gave a delighted giggle. "Well, in that case, I'd better make sure they're perfect," she murmured as she returned to her task.

Wade watched her for another minute, liking the fact that she wanted to look good for him, then turned another page of the newspaper. There was a write-up about that fellow Karl Leros—the one Hugh Rigel, who resembled Herman, had been talking about. There was a picture of Leros, too—a narrow-faced man in his early thirties with black hair and bushy eyebrows. Wade read the article, but it didn't say much more than what Rigel and Evan had told him.

"Wade?"

"Uh-huh?"

"Mark doesn't usually lock his car."

Wade looked over the top of the paper. Cass was staring reflectively at her hands and he couldn't make out her expression. "We're not talking about Mark."

She glanced up at him and batted her lashes. "Come on, I told you about my nail polish."

Wade didn't see the connection, but she seemed to think it was apparent. He sighed and gave up. "So. Mark doesn't lock his car. What of it?"

"Well . . ." She chewed on her lower lip. "He often leaves jackets in there. Couldn't the man have just left that jacket in his car?"

"In the winter?" Wade shook his head. "He'd be mighty conspicuous, honey."

"But he could have just switched jackets. Mark often left . . ."

Was this going to be another discussion about her image-reading ability? If so, Wade wasn't interested in having it. "Don't dwell on it," he advised. "No use stewing over things you can't do anything about."

Cass's mottled eyes sparkled at him. "You never know," she said softly. She bent her head to examine her hands and her cheeks which were stained pink.

Wade returned to his paper. Darn, he wished Evan would get on with locating Mark so Cassie could stop fretting herself about him. He didn't like to see her upset. As a matter of fact, it turned out that when she was upset, he was upset.

They'd spend tomorrow taking her mind off it. Cassie didn't have to work, and he didn't have to be on the base. He wasn't going to be there, either. He winced as he thought of the amount of work waiting for him, then shrugged it off. It had been some time since he'd spent an entire day away from his job and he was looking forward to it.

"I'm all done my nails," Cass announced. She jumped lightly to her feet and began unbuttoning her shirt while giving him one of her hot little looks. "I expect you to keep your eyes on them for at least an hour."

HE WASN'T going to be getting out of her system for quite some time.

Cass stood in the bathroom the next morning, brushing her hair and giving herself a good scolding. She should have known better than to let him move in with her like this. She should have known it would only make her feelings stronger, and it had.

He was simply too darn easy to live with. He effortlessly assumed all the everyday details that she was so poor at handling. Oh, he expected her to do her share, but he narrowed it down so she didn't have to wonder what to do next, and he did it in a manner that assumed she could handle it. "You make the toast while I do the eggs. You handle the dusting while I get on with the vacuuming." It was rather presumptuous, and very bossy, and . . . she liked it!

She liked everything about the man. He got up far too early, and caressed her until she was awake, as well, but it was nice opening her eyes and seeing his sensually narrowed eyes looking down into her face. It was nice having the coffee already made and the place tidy, and it was nice knowing she had the whole day to spend with him.

She heard the phone ring, moved automatically to answer it, then heard Wade bark out his version of a greeting. "Brillings!"

Cass rolled her eyes. It was probably a practical way to answer the phone, but she was going to try to train him to say "Hello" like a normal person. One of these days her mother would call, and Wade's bark would give the poor woman a heart attack. Of course, knowing her daughter had a male roommate would do the same thing, but there were more graceful ways of breaking that news than hearing Wade sound like a hit man. Then again, he wasn't going to be around long, so maybe that wouldn't happen.

Cass sat down on the edge of the bathtub and sighed. When Wade left, she would fall apart.

Don't think about it, she told herself. She had other more important things to worry about now.

She pulled a piece of paper out of the pocket of her walking shorts and studied it for about the millionth time. She had sketched a dark-haired man with bushy eyebrows, and although she hadn't had a lot of time, and although the image had been faded, she was positive this was the owner of the black suede jacket.

And maybe, instead of being a friend of Mark's, he was the man Wade and the police wanted to find.

She'd first had the idea last night, and she'd been turning it around in her mind ever since. This man didn't look like the usual computer types that Mark hung around with, and she'd certainly never seen him. Maybe he was a casual acquaintance, but if so, why would he leave his coat in Mark's car?

Maybe this black-suede-jacketed guy had traded coats! After all, Wade made it sound as if he'd been followed by some bad people. Maybe he'd wanted to disguise himself. Mark was always leaving coats in his car, and he never locked it, either. This man could have left that black suede jacket in Mark's car and put on one of Mark's.

There was no point in sharing this little idea with anyone. Wade wouldn't listen to her, and the police probably wouldn't, either. She was simply going to have to find out who he was herself. She should do something to get Mark out of this mess. She'd also like to prove to the police, and Wade and especially herself, that she was as capable as they were at dealing with practical realities.

Cass put the sketch back into her pocket and stood to check her appearance in the bathroom mirror. Cobalt-blue rayon walking shorts with a wide mauve inset, and a mauve sweater to match. Cobalt blue, to match Wade's eyes. She thought about him for a moment, then concentrated on the plans she'd made for today. She had the picture of the man. Now she needed his name and where he could be found. She had no idea how to go about getting that, but she bet Wade knew. She had all day with him. She'd ask him, very, very casually. Then she'd do it.

She had no intention of telling Wade what she had in mind and she wasn't going to tell him one thing about her adventure at Mark's last night, either. Listening to the police lecture had been bad enough. They had been very cross, although they'd accepted her story that she'd just stopped in to check the place. They had even grudgingly agreed she had every right to be in that house. She didn't think Wade would be as understanding.

Besides, Cass was nursing a tiny hope that if she solved this for him, he might realize he needed someone like her as much as she seemed to need him.

She gave her reflection an optimistic smile and opened the bathroom door.

Then she stopped smiling.

Wade was standing in the hall right outside the door, arms crossed, legs apart in his classic "I'm in charge" stance. His face was totally blank, and his eyes were hard slits of periwinkle blue. "All right, little lady," he snarled. "What in hell is going on?"

Cass took a quick look around. "I don't know. I was in here. I . . ."

Wade took her arm, marched her down the hall into the living room and pushed her onto the sofa. He stood in front of her and resumed his stance. "I just spoke with Evan," he snapped.

Cass studied his face, and her stomach gave a violent lurch. "Mark?" she whispered. She put a hand to her mouth. "Don't tell me they shot Mark!"

Wade shook his head. "No, honey, they haven't found him yet." He raised an eyebrow. "You wouldn't happen to know where he is, would you?"

"Me?" Cass was surprised at the question. "No."

"You spoke with him yesterday?"

"Yesterday?" What was this? "No. I wish I had, but—"

Wade's entire face scowled down at her. "Then what in God's name were you doing at his house last night?"

Cass sagged with dismay. Darn that Inspector McCleod! She really, really didn't want to have to explain this to Wade. She took a long breath and tried the same story she'd told the police. "I...uh...just stopped in to check on the place."

"I don't think so." Wade's voice hardened. "Mark contacted you, didn't he?"

Cass clapped a hand to her forehead and moaned. "What is the matter with you people?" she exclaimed. "I do one little thing and all you practical-reality folks jump to some bizarre conclusion I can't even follow." She looked back at him. "No, Wade, Mark did not contact me!"

"Then what were you doing at his house?" He didn't wait for an answer. "And don't give me that line about checking the place. You pulled a classic evasion on the police. You—"

"I didn't evade them," Cass said indignantly. "I accidentally lost them. I even pulled over and waited for them, but they didn't show up! I could hardly go back and ask them to start over."

Wade emitted a growl. "You trying to tell me you lost two professionals by accident?"

Cass shrugged a shoulder. "It's what happened."

He looked skeptical. "And then you just happened to decide to drop by Mark's house? After you realized they were gone, of course."

Cass considered it and nodded. "That's pretty much it."

For a long minute he just stood there, studying her out of those cold, expressionless eyes. "All right," he said softly. "We'll let that go. What happened when you got there?"

Cass winced and bent her head. "Didn't Inspector McCleod tell you all this?" she asked hopefully.

"Nope." Wade took a short breath. "He just said you'd been there, and he didn't want you there again. Apparently his men came real close to—" he took a breath "—to shooting you."

"No, they didn't," Cass objected. "They didn't even fire their guns. They were a little upset when I threw a lamp at one of them, but that wasn't all my fault. I didn't know they were policemen. It was too dark to see their clothes."

Wade's jaw tightened. "You attacked an armed man with a lamp?"

Cass examined her fingers. "I didn't really attack him. I just threw a lamp at him." She blinked up at him. "I missed."

"Oh, Christ!"

"Then one of them shouted 'police,' and switched on the lights, and I realized who they were and..." She sighed. "They weren't very happy about it." She gave him a tentative smile. "I let them follow me here, and I was very, very careful not to lose them."

Wade studied her in complete silence. "You are goddamn lucky the police in this city aren't trigger-happy," he finally said.

"I guess I am," Cass agreed. "I'll . . . uh . . . send them a thank-you card." She began to rise. "I should . . ."

"Why didn't you turn on the lights?" Wade asked.

Cass dropped back down and stared at him. "What?"

"The lights, Cassie." His scowl darkened. "You stopped by to check on a house and didn't turn the lights on? Doesn't sound like someone checking a house to me. Not only that, but you never mentioned this last night." He produced his snarl. "If it was all so innocent, I think you would have told me about it, don't you?"

"Not really," Cass muttered. She shook back her hair and lifted her chin and stared him straight in the eye. "It's none of your concern, Wade."

For a moment Wade just stared back at her with amazement on his face. Then his expression changed to a dangerous hardness that reminded her of the way he'd looked when she'd first seen him in her store. "You put yourself in a potentially dangerous situation, and it's none of my concern?"

"That's right," Cass said firmly. "I don't have to tell you every little move I make."

"Little move?" Wade roared. "I don't call sneaking into that house and almost getting shot a 'little move.' I want to know what you were doing there, and you're going to tell me. Now!"

Cass watched him settle more firmly into his stance and gave up. He'd badger this out of her one way or another. "Oh, all right," she said crossly. She took a long breath and looked straight into the frozen slits of periwinkle blue. "I went there to get a reading off that black suede jacket."

"You *what?*"

"I just wanted to know who it belonged to," Cass went on. "You're all hunting for the wrong man, and—"

Wade's voice became dangerously soft. "You went there because of this idiotic notion you've got that you're psychic?"

"It's not idiotic," Cass insisted. "I can do it. You're just too practical to believe me, which is why I didn't tell you about it in the first place." She tugged the sketch out of her pocket. "I even made a drawing of the jacket owner."

Wade snatched it out of her hand, stared at it and then back at her.

"I don't know who he is," Cass continued on. "He might be one of Mark's friends, or he could be the man you were supposed to meet. He could be, Wade. Mark is always leaving jackets in his car and maybe—"

"Leros," Wade interrupted. "His name is Karl Leros and his picture is in that newspaper right there."

Cass pushed aside the papers on the coffee table and found the newspaper. There he was, right corner, front page. She felt a huge burst of triumph and relief. Now she didn't have to go searching for him. Now Wade had to believe her!

She gazed expectantly up at his face, but he didn't seem to be getting it. "Well, there it is then," she stated. "He's the man who owns that jacket. He . . ."

"He was killed in a car accident!" Wade tossed the sketch onto the coffee table.

Cass looked back down at the newspaper and scanned the article. "Maybe he's not the right man then. He sure resembled him, though. And there was that cold, creepy feeling when I touched the jacket."

"Oh, for God's sake . . ."

"I could be wrong," Cass admitted. "There wasn't much time and . . . and then there were the police. I'll go back to the house and get another reading and we can—"

"You'll do no such thing!" Wade thundered. "You will forget about this nonsense and stay the hell out of it!"

Cass glared at him. "It's not nonsense. And I'm just trying to help. I—"

"Help?" He shook his head. "We don't need your help! You've got too much imagination and too little common sense, Cassie. You stick to dressmaking and leave this investigation to people who know how to go about it!"

Cass just sat there and stared at him. There it was again, the dreaded "too" word that told her she just didn't measure up. And she'd been right when she'd thought hearing him say it would be horrible. It was. She was, after all, "too" something for him. And of course he didn't need her. He never would. She was foolish even to have hoped it would be different this time.

Suddenly she was furious with him. She'd told him she was too impractical and he'd said it didn't matter.

He'd just walked around being wonderful and she'd fallen in love with him, and he didn't care enough about her to try to understand anything.

"Of course I'm too imaginative," she said softly. "I certainly have too much imagination for you, because you don't have any!" She bounced to her feet. "And I am really, really tired of all you practical people deciding how much of everything is the right amount of something. As far as I'm concerned, most of you don't have enough of anything except for common sense and then you've got too much!"

"Don't you start ranting at me," Wade warned. "I can't tolerate—"

"There are too many things you can't tolerate," Cass interrupted. "If you expect your dates to remember them all, I suggest you make a list!"

"What the hell are you—"

"I'm not the only one who's 'too' something, you know," Cass went on. "You are too . . . intolerant You are also too stubborn, too unimaginative and too . . . a whole bunch of other things that I don't tolerate!" She glanced around for her purse and snatched it off the floor. "I'll go to my store and do something I'm good at doing and you can get your things and go. I'm too impractical for you and you are far, far too practical for me." She gave him one long, last miserable look. "And you should stop on your way back to the base and pick up a cellular phone. You and that dreadful Inspector McCleod person can talk to each other all day on it. It's just the sort of thing you practical people do with your time!"

WADE DROPPED into a chair with a bright-fuchsia cushion and listened to Cass's car drive away. He took long, deep breaths to cool down his temper.

Lord, he was furious with her! How in hell could she have been so foolish as to sneak into that house and almost get herself shot? He shuddered at the idea. Christ, when Evan had told him what had happened, he'd been grateful he was sitting down. He'd assumed she'd put herself in that position because of Mark, and he could to some extent understand it. When he'd realized it was because of her ridiculous image-reading notions he'd wanted to chew her out until she was a cowering, agreeable little bundle who'd promise never, ever to put herself in that position again.

Instead, she'd come right back at him. What the hell was wrong with women, anyway? They were supposed to sit still and listen for their own good, not go into some long-winded rant about his faults.

They weren't supposed to walk out of his life, either.

That's what she'd done. She'd told him to take his things and go away. Well, that's what he wanted to do, too. He got to his feet and stomped down to the bedroom to pack, gritting his teeth against the cold knot that was forming in his stomach. Okay, there had been some things he'd enjoyed about the experience. The sex had been great. She had been good company, and he'd liked watching her trying to decide what to wear, and he'd liked trying to figure out how her mind worked and wondering what she'd say next and . . .

He shook his head and went into the bathroom to get his shaving things, trying not to look at the bottles of perfume and nail polish and makeup strewn across the counter. It could be that he'd become a bit accustomed to having a woman around. Nothing to concern himself about. If he found he wanted one, he could always get another one. Not one like Cassie, of course. One without too much imagination. One who had a lot of common sense, and not as many clothes and who didn't go throwing herself at car thieves or sneaking into a house because she thought she could read an image off a jacket. He grimaced at the idea of being with someone else. Somehow, he couldn't see himself with anyone but her.

He carried his bag to the front, fighting an overwhelming feeling of panic. The affair with Cassie was going to end anyway. He hadn't wanted it to end this soon, that's all. In spite of her illogical actions and those insults she'd hurled at him, she still wasn't out of his system. It would have taken all the time he had left in Calgary for that to happen. Even then, he'd probably be feeling like this, as if a vital body organ had been removed.

Maybe if he could have had six months. A year?

Actually, when he thought about it, he knew that wouldn't have been long enough, either. He'd need a lot longer than that. A couple of centuries, maybe.

He dropped into a chair and finally admitted it. Evan was right. Cassie wasn't going to be getting out of his system. She'd snuck under his skin in a way he hadn't anticipated and she was there to stay. Without her, his life would be drab and colorless and uninteresting.

Damn! Now what was he going to do? She'd told him to get out, and that look in her eyes told him she'd meant it. She'd said he was all wrong for her. Too intolerant. Too unimaginative. Too stubborn. They didn't sound like faults to him, but apparently she thought they were.

He glared at the sketch she'd made, which was still sitting on the coffee table. That's what had started this whole thing. He picked it up. It was a good rendition of Leros. She must have seen his picture in the newspaper, decided he was the type to wear a black suede jacket and subconsciously merged the two ideas. Illogical, of course, but perhaps he could have been more tolerant about it. Used his imagination a little. Been not quite so stubborn. Of course, he'd been doing it for her own good, but that was beside the point. She was in no mood to see that now.

He climbed to his feet. He'd better get good at dealing with women in a real hurry.

Otherwise a black suede jacket might just have ruined the rest of his life.

# 12

"My men were just a few minutes behind her," Evan said apologetically. "We never expected her to take off like that. Maybe we should have, but . . ."

"She didn't take off," Wade growled between his teeth. "She was taken off." He stomped around in the snowy alley behind Cassie's store, and literally ordered his heart to keep on beating. He was covered in a cold sweat, and his stomach was knotted with something he hadn't felt for years.

Fear.

It was even worse than fear. It was an almost mind-numbing terror. He was terrified about what might have already happened to her, and he was terrified at what it would do to him if it had.

He'd come up with the perfect plan. He'd driven to Mark's house to pick up the black suede jacket, and he was going to have Cass do her image-reading thing from it again. Then he would take whatever she said as God's honest truth and follow up on it. That should keep her from ranting at him and give him time to con her back to her place and into the bedroom. There he could make love to her until that admiring look was back in her eyes. The minute he saw it, he'd tell her how things were going to be.

It was a good plan, one he was anxious to put into effect. But when he'd arrived at the store, there was no sign of her. The Pontiac she'd been driving was parked where she usually parked, but she wasn't inside, and the tracks in the snow suggested she hadn't made it that far.

Those tracks in the snow were the reason that Wade had broken into the store to call Evan and order him over there, pronto. "It's all here," he explained now, and he was impressed with how cool his voice sounded. "She pulled up in that Pontiac, got out and walked to the door. Another car—something heavy, an Olds I suspect—pulled in behind her. Two men got out and grabbed her." He pressed his lips together at the mental picture this story was creating. "She put up one hell of a fight, but they dragged her around to the back of their car and tossed her into the trunk." He tried not to think about how unpleasant that had been for her. She was a gutsy little lady. She'd handle it until he got there. *Hang on, baby,* he mentally assured her. *I'll find you.*

She wouldn't know he was searching for her. She wouldn't know anyone even knew she had a problem. Christ, she must be as terrified as he was.

He examined the tracks again to make sure he hadn't missed anything, then focused back on Evan.

The RCMP officer was standing very still, his hands shoved in his pockets and his head bent while he stared at the ground. "That is what it looks like," he nodded. He glanced up with an unreadable expression. "Or she could have gone willingly. Maybe Dowling contacted her and—"

"That's not what happened," Wade snapped. "Someone took her." He drew in a long breath of cold winter air. "It's probably Orion's group. They'll think she knows something about Dowling, and when she doesn't . . ." He gritted his teeth and glowered at Evan. "I want her found, damn it!"

Evan's gray eyes narrowed. "So do I, Commander. We're doing everything we can to locate her, but we don't have a lot to go on. No one around here saw anything. My men didn't see anything. We can't stop every Olds in town and check the trunk, so unless you've got a brilliant idea . . ."

Brilliant idea? He didn't have one single idea, and he felt so damn responsible for this. He should have known better than to start chewing her out. He should have just humored her along and told her he believed her image-reading thing and . . .

He paused and considered it. She'd drawn a sketch that looked exactly like Leros, and she'd been so sure she was right. Why would she pick Leros? Leros had been wearing a ski jacket when he died—could he have pulled it out of Mark's car? Wade had a brief flash of Hugh Rigel sitting nervously in his office and looking warily at Wade. If Cassie was right, then Hugh Rigel's little visit the other day would be mighty suspicious, wouldn't it?

It wasn't much to go on, and there was a good chance it was just a red herring, but it was certainly better than nothing. "Rigel," he said. "Hugh Rigel. What do you have on him?"

WHOEVER OWNED this place had a lot of money, Cass decided. Unfortunately, the person also had appallingly bad taste.

She sat on a black leather chair in what appeared to be an office, and tried very hard to concentrate on the decor. She quite liked the massive rosewood desk and the matching bookshelves, but the rest of the room definitely needed help. The walls were darkly paneled, the carpet was brown and all the furniture was black leather. It was really quite grim.

So were the other occupants of the room—two tough-looking men beside her, each with a gun in his hand. The guns were aimed right at her. They obviously didn't know her well, or they'd know she was extremely harmless.

She didn't know much about them, except that they weren't policemen, and she'd realized that too late. She'd been numb from her fight with Wade and all she'd wanted to do was get into her store and lose herself in her work.

When the car had turned into the alley behind her, she hadn't been worried. She'd even stood by her door, waiting, as the men got out. It wasn't until they neared her that she'd suddenly understood that the black-haired man had on a dark-blue down jacket that was about four years old, and she'd remembered the man who'd attacked her at Mark's house. But it was far too late. There had been a futile little wrestling match, which she had lost, followed by an unpleasant ride in the trunk of a car. Finally, she'd been dragged out of that, into this very posh, three-story house in the middle of nowhere. She had no idea why she'd been brought here, but it was a good bet that it wasn't for a fashion consultation.

She called up a mental image of Wade and concentrated on his face. Mr. Tough-Guy. He'd be able to handle this. Then again, he'd never get himself into a situation like this. At least thinking about him made her feel less scared. It did make her feel like crying, though.

Cass couldn't think of anything to say to her captors; she couldn't think of anything to do, either. She felt as if she would throw up any minute, and there was a dreadful dull ache where her heart used to be. She leaned back against the uncomfortable leather upholstery and wished these men would go away so she could be miserable alone.

"Miss Lloyd!" exclaimed a cranky voice. "It's certainly time we met, isn't it?"

Cass opened her eyes and glanced toward the wide, arched entrance to the room. A small, overweight man with a round, unsmiling face came through it, accompanied by a tall, heavyset man with pale-gray eyes, dressed in a black suit. The smaller man wore a pair of brown trousers and a darker brown sweater—both expensive name brands. They couldn't disguise his rotund build or his jerky way of walking, which was rather reminiscent of Herman moving about his cage.

Except Herman never looked like he was ready to throttle her. This man did. He settled his brown-clad body into the leather chair behind the desk and glared at her out of nasty-looking brown eyes.

"I'm Hugh Rigel," he announced. He motioned toward his large companion. "This is Walter and you've already met Roger and Conner." He nodded in the direction of the two gun-wielding men, then glowered at her again. "I'm sure you know what I want."

Cass felt a headache coming on. "I certainly don't!" she informed him. "I don't like being dragged around like this and I really don't like men with guns, so if you don't mind—"

"I don't have time for this," he interjected. "I have a buyer lined up, and—"

"A buyer?" Hugh Rigel was a salesman? "I certainly hope you aren't bringing a customer here in the trunk of a car. It doesn't put anyone in a good mood. It is also very hard on your clothes."

Rigel gaped at her for a minute, then let out a short, humorless bark of laughter. "You are good, aren't you? I admire that, although it has cost me a lot of trouble." He tapped his short, chubby fingers together. "Perhaps it would help if I told you that I'm better known as Orion. Or did you discern that already?"

"Not really." Cass took a few deep breaths. Orion. That was the name of the weapons smuggler everyone thought Mark worked for. She began to feel a bit more cheerful. Gracious, she was going to solve this mystery, wasn't she? Her spirits dropped again. She might solve it, but she might not live through it. No one would even know she had a problem. She'd just kicked Wade out of her life, the store wasn't open, no one would realize she was missing until Monday. She was on her own.

It wasn't a very uplifting thought.

Rigel leaned back in his chair and blinked his round brown eyes at her. "I know what you've been doing, Miss Lloyd, although I had no idea who you were until my men picked you up today."

"Oh?" Cass murmured. He knew she'd just broken up with Wade?

"It was you Karl Leros met Monday night, wasn't it? I thought it was Brillings, but he doesn't know anything." He smiled with satisfaction. "I even went to see him, just to make certain."

Karl Leros! That was the man in the newspaper. The man who owned the black suede jacket. Had she been right about that?

"We followed Leros to that parking lot, and after a while he talked." Rigel shrugged a shoulder. "He didn't enjoy the experience, Miss Lloyd, and you won't, either."

"That so?" Cass said in her best Wade imitation. What on earth was this man going on and on about?

"He told us he dumped his jacket and the item in the back seat of a Camaro in that rapid-transit parking lot. We went back to pick it up, but you showed up, along with Brillings. Good trick, using him for backup. Worked like a charm, didn't it?"

"Actually, it did," Cass agreed. Jacket, he'd said. She had been right! Too bad no one had believed her. And

what was this item he'd mentioned? She had a brief
flash of the gray box she'd put in Herman's cage. Good
grief, was that the weapon sort of thing they thought
Mark was smuggling? And she'd had that all the time?
*Oh, Wade, I'm ever-so sorry,* she thought. *I should have
known when you told me. How dumb can I be?* Of
course, they could make it easier by putting a label on
it.

"Well, my dear, we have been looking for you ever
since. You did a good job of vanishing. We connected
you with someone named Mark Dowling, but there
wasn't anything in his house to suggest who you were.
Nothing in his office, either." Rigel shook his head. "We
thought that sooner or later you'd return to his house,
and you finally did last night. We followed you, but we
had to wait until you were alone before picking you up.
By the way, did you know that the police are watching
you?"

Cass nodded without speaking. It was just dawning
on her that these people were under the impression she
was some sort of spy.

He chuckled. "I thought you must. You've also got
Brillings living with you. I assume you're pulling some
sort of double-cross on him."

Double cross? Wade? Did this man actually think she
was smart enough to do that? Or stupid enough to try?

Rigel leaned his fat little body forward. "Who are you
working for, Miss Lloyd?"

Cass was almost positive he wasn't asking for the name of her store. "I'm sort of . . . uh . . . free-lancing," she told him. It wasn't really a lie.

Rigel considered that, then shrugged. "It doesn't really matter. I just want my item back. If you've already sold it, I want to know who you sold it to, but I don't believe you have." He settled back in his chair. "Now, where is it?"

Cass stared at him. She couldn't tell them it was in Herman's cage! They might hurt Herman. Besides, Wade wanted it, and she'd rather give it to him, although she wasn't certain she'd get the chance. She had a tiny little suspicion that once this fellow had that gray box thing, he wouldn't need her.

Rigel remained silent for a minute, then sighed. "I realize you do not want to tell us, but it would be more comfortable for you if you did." He glanced up at the big man beside him. "Walter very much enjoys using his knife."

Cass watched Walter pull something very nasty-looking out of his pocket, and shuddered. Now what? She was too scared to think of a way out of this. She needed some time to come up with a plan. Let's see, they'd searched Mark's house. She didn't want them at her place. Maybe they would accidentally set off the alarms in her store. "It's at Creative Elegance," she lied. "That's the store I've been using as a—" what the heck was the word "—a front." She tried to think of some place in the store they couldn't wreck. "It's in the bottom right drawer in the long, white workbench. In a...uh..." What did spies use? "A hidden compartment at the back."

"Very clever." Rigel nodded.

Cass almost let her jaw drop. The first time someone thought she was clever and it was a creep like this. "Thank you," she murmured.

Rigel turned to Walter. "Send a couple of men to pick it up as soon as it's dark. Tell them to watch out for Brillings. I don't want him to start sniffing this out." He turned back to the men guarding her. "Put her into the storage room in the basement and keep an eye on her." He smiled grimly at Cass. "As soon as we have the item in our possession, we can discuss your future."

One of the men gestured with his gun and Cass rose uneasily to her feet.

Wade had said there were one thousand and one common household items that could be used as a weapon. She sure hoped she would find a couple in Mr. Rigel's storeroom.

Too bad she hadn't asked Wade to make a list.

"THIS IS like a guessing game," Cass muttered. "I've never been any good at those." She gave the screw in the towel rack one last turn with her nail file, then pulled the rack away from the wall, flushing the toilet at the same time to disguise any noise.

She held her treasure up for examination. It was actually a very nice brass towel rack, but it didn't look very dangerous. Was a towel rack on Wade's list?

If not, too bad. Cass had no other ideas. There wasn't anything at all in that storeroom, and after being shut up there for four hours, she'd had enough of the place. It was cold, dirty, smelly and damp, and there was nothing to do in there but imagine how awful it was going to be having Walter use his knife on her, or replay the last scene with Wade over and over and over. She knew it was getting dark outside, and it wouldn't be long before Rigel realized she hadn't told him the truth. She simply had to leave before that happened.

Finally, she'd requested a washroom break at the top of her lungs, and Roger had appeared and dragged her in here. Now he was on the other side of that door, he had a gun, and heaven knows how many other men like him there were in the house. Her brief escape attempt could end very badly, but Cass refused to think about that. There was a time for practicality and this wasn't it.

She took a long look at her reflection in the bathroom mirror. White face; wide staring eyes; walking shorts with a rip in them; a towel rack in her right hand. Not exactly a sinister image, was it?

Roger tapped on the door. "That's long enough!" he ordered, and the door handle began to turn.

It was now or never. Cass held the towel rack down by her right side and took a long, deep breath. "I can't do up my zipper," she announced plaintively as the door swung open.

Roger leered offendingly, took a step into the bathroom, and Cass swung. The towel rack connected with his midriff, he grunted with surprise and bent forward and she hit him again on the back of the head. He dropped to the floor, and the gun slid out of his fingers.

Cass stared down at him. Good heavens, she'd never expected to knock him out. She started to step over him, then stopped. A gun was probably better than a towel rack as a weapon. She gingerly picked it up. It was surprisingly heavy, and she had use to both hands to hold it. If she had known this was going to happen, she would have asked Wade to show her how to use it. Did you have to do anything special, or just pull the trigger? She took a moment to examine it, pulled back on the hammerlike piece to peek inside, and heard it click. Good. That must mean it worked.

She slid out of the door into the hallway and paused. To the left was that storage room and she wasn't going there. She tried to remember the layout. There had been stairs and a short hall and a bedroom . . . She turned to the right, saw the staircase and froze.

Walter stood at the bottom of the stairs, staring at her as if he couldn't believe his eyes. Then his mouth lifted in a snarl and he started for her.

Cass raised her hands and pointed the gun at him. "Y-you stay away from me," she ordered. Both her voice and her hands shook, and naturally, Walter, like everyone else, didn't take her seriously.

Instead he laughed. He actually laughed at her.

"Give me that thing," he said contemptuously, and he kept coming. "It doesn't look like you know what to do with it."

Now even the bad guys were telling her she was incompetent! "You're right," Cass agreed. "I don't." She aimed the gun over his head and gave the trigger a gentle squeeze. "But I'm not so impractical I'd just hand it over to you."

She hadn't intended to fire the thing. She'd thought it would just click again, but it didn't. It sort of exploded, and she staggered back and the ceiling began to rain plaster down on Walter, who was standing very still and staring at her with total amazement.

Cass waved the gun in his direction, her breath coming in short, surprised pants. "Now, you should . . . uh . . ."

She didn't get a chance to finish the sentence. For no reason whatsoever, Walter crumpled in slow motion and lay very still on the floor.

Cass stared down at him. Good grief, she hadn't shot him had, she? She looked back up, and gasped.

The shadows on the staircase behind Walter were shifting, moving, transforming into a big, heartbreakingly familiar male figure. Cass blinked at him a couple of times, then said the first thing that came into her head. "Good heavens, Wade, what on earth are you wearing?"

HUGH RIGEL'S STUDY looked a lot better with Wade in it.

Cass sat on one of the black leather chairs and

watched him. He was standing talking to Evan Mc-
Cleod and eyeing her with that familiar unfathomable
expression of his. He had on black pants and a black
turtleneck, and except for the black toque and radio
headset he'd removed, he looked very much as he had
when she'd encountered him on the staircase about
twenty minutes ago. Tough. Controlled. And very,
very sexy.

She still had absolutely no idea where he'd come from
or what he was doing there. He'd just materialized on
the stairs, and had mumbled something into that radio
thing about finding her. Then the house had filled with
police and he'd ignored them and brought her up here,
and pulled her into his lap and held her tight, while his
big body trembled underneath her and she tried to explain what had happened. He hadn't seemed particularly interested, even when she'd told him about the
gray box in Herman's cage. He'd just grunted that he'd
check into it, and had gone on holding her.

Finally Evan had summoned him away for a little
chat, and he'd sighed and gone. At least he looked more
like himself now, although his face was still a bit pale
under that tan. Perhaps he shouldn't go around having
adventures like this.

He shook Evan's hand and strolled across the room
toward her, and Cass sucked in her bottom lip. Nothing had changed since this morning, she reminded herself. They weren't suited—they never would be, and she

wasn't going to be impractical enough to daydream about him anymore.

He crouched in front of her and frowned. "I'm going to have to get out of here, honey. This is going to be big news. The media are on the way, and I'm not one of those people who like their picture in the paper, if you get my meaning." He raised an eyebrow. "You think you can cope with this crowd all on your own?"

"I'll be fine, thank you," Cass said politely. Was this goodbye? She wished she didn't have to say it with all these people around. She swallowed hard and looked into his eyes. Cobalt blue, she noted. She looked away. "Thank you for...uh...taking care of Walter down there."

"I should have been here sooner," he complained, "but Evan wouldn't let me out of his sight. Said he didn't need some half-crazed ex-commando blowing up good portions of Alberta." He smiled slightly. "Sounded good to me, but Canadian police are peculiar about things like that."

"How odd," Cass responded. Was she ever going to be involved in a conversation she understood?

"Well, they are civilians," he said, as if that explained everything. He put one big hand on her cheek. "We wouldn't have found you at all if it hadn't been for that jacket."

"Jacket?" Cass repeated faintly. "What...?"

"The black suede one." He put on his slow, coaxing smile. "After I got over being intolerant, unimaginative and stubborn I realized you might just be on to something."

Cass's cheeks warmed. "You recovered from that, did you?"

"In one hell of a hurry. As soon as I realized something had happened to you." He bent his head, and when he lifted it his face appeared almost gray and very grim. "It's the only clue I had." He nodded in Evan's direction. "He was pretty open-minded about it, all things considered. We started checking into Leros's death and found a few strange things and then we latched onto Rigel. At first it didn't look real good—Rigel has covered things up well—but Evan got most of the police force in North America working on it. I had to keep at him, of course, but . . ."

It suddenly hit Cass what he was saying. "You mean . . . you got all these people here and you . . . you bothered all the policemen in Canada just because of me and . . . and what I said about that black suede jacket?"

"Uh-huh. You really can do that, can't you?"

Cass nodded silently, too choked up to speak.

He looked deeply into her eyes. "And when you touched my medallion, you saw an image of me in my uniform?"

"That's right." She blinked dreamily at his tough, sexy face. He'd finally believed her; he'd probably antagonized half the police force in the country just to find her, and he'd come rushing out to save her. "Oh,

Wade," she whispered. "It's no wonder I love you so much."

His eyes blazed cobalt blue heat and he leaned forward and brushed his lips over hers and pressed something into her hand. "We'll settle this later," he announced as he got to his feet. He turned toward the door.

Cass stared after him, then glanced down at the object in her hand.

It was a round, silver medallion on a long, silver chain.

# 13

"AND THIS is a copy of my itinerary," Mark concluded. He pulled a piece of paper out of the pocket of his red-and-black down jacket and set it on the sewing table.

"Thank you." Cass smiled up into his square, rather puzzled-looking face. "You will phone tomorrow when you get to your hotel?"

"Yeah, sure." Mark sat on the edge of the sewing table and examined her with a somewhat bewildered expression. "Do I have to keep doing this ... like ... forever?"

Cass bent her head and concentrated hard on the suit she was making—a lovely gray-and-mauve wool creation for a new customer. "What do you mean?"

"Well, it's just that ... ever since I got snowed in by that blizzard three weeks ago, you've been acting kind of ... bizarre. I mean, I can hardly go to the bathroom without phoning you." He pouted down his lips. "And when I went out the other night and didn't tell you, you *yelled* at me."

"I didn't yell at you," Cass objected. "Besides, even if I did, you deserved it. Really, Mark, you have to live more practically. You can't take off without telling someone where you're going. It's simply not realistic."

"Realistic?"

"That's right. And . . . and I don't want to hear any more about it."

Mark stared at her in stunned silence, then cleared his throat. "Uh . . . okay." He coughed again. "How about Herman? He hasn't been back at my place."

"It's too cold out for Herman to be moved," Cass said quickly. She didn't even want to think about her house without Herman there. Perhaps she should get a hamster of her own, although Herman was rather special. After all, they'd been through a lot together. "Besides, you're going out of town again. It's much more practical for him to be at my place." She gave Mark a little smile. "You're welcome to come and visit."

"Right. Well, uh, I guess you don't want my car, do you?"

Cass shook her head. "I don't do cars anymore, Mark, thank you. I'm fine on the bus. Really."

She walked Mark to the back door and hugged him too long. "Remember to phone," she ordered. He studied her face with obvious concern and she forced a small, reassuring smile. "I know I'm acting a bit strangely, but I'm sure I'll get over it soon."

She returned to her workbench and sat down in her chair. That wasn't true at all. She was no nearer getting over it than she had been three weeks ago. *Darn you, Wade*, she thought as she returned to her seat. She checked the seam she was sewing, then hesitated. "No," she said out loud. "Yesterday you decided not to do that anymore." She glanced at her purse. Then again, once more couldn't hurt. She opened her purse and pulled out the silver medallion she'd found in the snow at the Brentwood parking lot.

She set the medallion on her lap and sighed. This was the only way she'd seen Wade since he'd strode out of Hugh Rigel's house three weeks ago. He hadn't been at her place when she'd finally gotten home that night, but she'd known he wouldn't be. Evan McCleod had explained it to her. Commander Brillings had been ordered back to the States immediately, to keep his involvement in this as quiet as possible. He'd taken that gray box with him, which was some sort of weapon prototype stolen from an American research station.

So why was she still mooning over this medallion? If she had any practicality at all in her, she'd put it away somewhere and get on with her life. Wade obviously realized she'd been right, that they didn't have a thing in common, and she was probably well out of his system by now.

Unfortunately he wasn't out of hers. She picked up the medallion, closed her fingers around it and shut her eyes.

The heat started from her fingertips and wound its way up her arm. The image hadn't changed. In front of her closed eyes was a big man with a blunt-nosed face, summer-sky eyes, sandy-red hair and full sensuous lips—the man she loved.

"Hi, honey," drawled a familiar voice.

Cass gasped, jumped to her feet and whirled around.

The image she had just seen had come to life and was standing in her store. He had on a pair of blue jeans—

Levi's this time—and that familiar denim jacket with the sheepskin lining. The store was filled with his male scent, the room constricted with his large presence and Cass's heart stopped beating entirely. She blinked a few times. "Wade?"

"Uh-huh." He studied her up and down with that expressionless look of his, then took two quick strides toward her and pulled her into his arms for a hard, swift kiss. Then he stepped back, keeping his hands wrapped around her forearms, and looked searchingly into her face. "How've you been?"

"F-fine," Cass stuttered. Was he really here or was she having some sort of hallucination?

"Police didn't give you a bad time, did they?"

Cass couldn't stop staring at him. He was just as sexy and tough and cool as always, and she loved him every bit as much as she had three weeks ago. She just wished he wouldn't act as if they were in the middle of a conversation, and tell her what he was doing here. "Police?" she repeated.

"At Rigel's house," he said impatiently. "Did they...?"

"They were very nice," Cass interjected. Did he know that was three weeks ago? From the way he was behaving, it appeared he thought it was last night. "What are you doing here?"

"Got some forms for you to sign." He eased her back into her chair. "You best sit down, honey. You look a mite shook up."

Cass blinked rapidly and took a few long breaths. She'd been miserable without him, and he'd just stopped by to get her to sign some papers? "Forms?"

"Uh-huh." He flicked open his jacket, revealing his olive green, cable-knit sweater, and grinned at her. "Found myself in a green mood this morning," he announced, straight-faced. He pulled a raft of folded papers out of the inside pocket of his jacket and unfolded them. "I've got a ton of paperwork for you to sign. It's mostly military stuff." He set a form in front of her and handed her a pen. "Sign right here."

Cass glanced down at the page, then back up at him. Of course! She should have known he'd have a practical reason for being here.

She swallowed the lump in her throat and tried to concentrate on the form. It was an official-looking document of some sort with a number in bold type on the right-hand corner. "What is this?"

"Just standard procedure." Wade patted her shoulder. "It's always like this. You'll get used to it. They just like a lot of things in triplicate. I have no idea what they do with all of them."

It didn't make any sense, but it was probably something to do with Orion and that secret weapon she'd kept in Herman's cage. "Shouldn't I, uh, read it first?"

"Go ahead," Wade invited. "It's not all that necessary, though. I've been over them two or three dozen times and I don't see any problem."

Cass tried to read it, but the words just blurred in front of her. This was horrible. She'd just sign this thing and then maybe he'd go away, and maybe she'd finally get over him and . . . She wrote her name.

"And here," Wade prompted. He took it and replaced it with another one. "This one you have to sign beside my name, then initial down here. Uh-huh. And here."

Even his handwriting was practical. A straight W. J. Brillings that looked very stern beside her own swirls. Cass forced her hand to write.

"That's good," he said approvingly, as he took that paper away and set a couple more in front of her. "This is because it's international. Turns out to complicate things a little. There're four places here."

"International?" Cass mumbled.

"Uh-huh. You being a Canadian citizen and all. The next one is the security-check authorization. They already did it, as a personal favor to me, but you still have to . . ."

Cass hesitated. "Why do I need a security check?"

"Standard procedure," Wade grunted. "Sign there. It's a little more complicated because I'm involved. They're real particular about who folks in my position are marrying. Initial there. And right—"

Cass froze, with the pen suspended over the line. "Marrying?" She glanced up at him. Had he just said that? "Who is getting married?"

Wade looked at her as if she'd lost her mind. "We are, baby. You and I."

The knot in Cass's throat loosened just a little. Was he serious? She examined his face, but he didn't appear to be joking. He looked quite matter-of-fact about it. Had she missed something here? "Y-you think we're getting married?"

"Uh-huh."

"But . . ." She blinked rapidly. "But I haven't seen or heard from you for three weeks and . . ."

"That wasn't my choice," Wade said, scowling. "There were a few loose ends to clean up after Rigel's capture. I've got to go where I'm sent, Cassie. I can't tell you where it was, but you can be sure there wasn't a phone I could use." He tapped the page. "Sign here, and then we're all through."

Cass reached for the pen, then realized what she was doing and stopped. It wasn't that she didn't like the idea of being married to him. She did, very much. But it would only end in disaster, like her other encounters with him. She wasn't impractical enough to do that to herself again. She shook her head. "No."

"No?" Wade repeated. He folded his arms and frowned down at her. "What are you talking about? You said you loved me. When a woman says that, well, it's time to get married. You did and we are."

"But . . ." Cass moistened her lips. "But that was three weeks ago."

He shut his eyes and took a long breath. "You'll feel that way again," he said, almost to himself. He raised his eyelids and studied her with grim determination. "It's just that you haven't seen me for a while, that's all. We'll spend some time together and—"

"No, we won't," Cass said decisively. She pushed herself to her feet and backed away from him. "I don't know why you're doing this, but we both know it wouldn't work. I'm too imaginative for you, remember. I don't have enough common sense and I'm not going to let you break my heart again just because I was so impractical that I fell in love with you."

He grinned widely and his eyes gleamed with triumph. "So you still do love me?"

"Yes, of course I do, but that—"

"Good." He let out his breath in a long, relieved sigh. "You had me going there. Now, sit back down, honey, and finish signing these things."

What was it with this man? Did he only hear what he wanted to hear? "No! It is not a realistic thing to do."

"It's the only realistic thing to do!" He glowered at her. "I can't damn well be without you, Cassie."

Cass gaped at him. "You can't?"

"No, I can't." He reached out, grabbed her wrist and yanked her up against his hard, hot body. "Now, I'm not saying we won't have a few problems, but there shouldn't be that many. We already know the sex is good. Moneywise, well, I've got a salary that can support us both, but you go right on working if you've a mind to do it. I don't suppose you'd let me stop you anyway."

"Probably not, but . . ."

"We never got around to discussing kids," he said thoughtfully. "I wouldn't mind a few, but we'll have to think on it. And not just yet. Going to be a little while before I'm ready to share you with youngsters. I'm not wild about the name Evan, either, but if it's your choice, I'll accept it."

"Evan?" Cass repeated. A slow, delicious thrill that began in her toes was moving up her body. He'd given this quite a lot of thought, hadn't he? Maybe . . .

He went on. "Your family is going to be a little farther away, but I'll make sure you get to see them as least as often as you do now." He gestured around the shop. "As to this place, well, there's just no way you can keep it." He held up a hand. "I know that's a hardship for you, but I can't do much about it. We'll discuss the business details with your partner and see what we can work out. I've done some research in Washington and there is plenty of opportunity if you want to open up a place like this down there."

"Washington?"

"That's where we'll be living." He brushed a finger down her cheek. "I don't have a place yet. I'm not the one who should pick out something like that. We'll do it together. I've got a new assignment that shouldn't involve all that much traveling, although there will be some." He lowered his eyebrows. "But when I'm gone, baby, I'm going to make sure that place is filled with so goddamn much stuff of mine that you can't set down a hand without thinking about me."

Cass's entire body shivered with delight at the images his words were creating. *Now, hang on*, she cautioned herself. This was exactly the same method he'd used to convince her to sleep with him. She studied him with sudden wariness. "That sounds . . . interesting but . . . um . . . a bit more like a military takeover than a marriage proposal."

"A military takeover is a hell of lot easier," Wade grumbled. "Look, Cassie, you've got no reason to say no. You love me, and you must know I feel the same way about you. I've been so miserable without you the past three weeks I could hardly stand being in the same room with myself."

Cass studied his face and put a hand on his cheek. "Oh, Wade," she whispered. "Do you really feel that way?"

"Of course I do," he said impatiently. "As for this practicality stuff you keep going on and on about, I don't see that it's a problem. I have too much of it and you don't have enough, so it seems to me it ought to even itself out. Now, are you going to keep arguing, or can we get on with it?"

Cass gave herself one minute to consider it, but stopped after ten seconds, threw her arms around his neck and pressed her lips to his. She wasn't so impractical that she'd give up this.

Besides, she was eager to try her designs on the military crowd. Perhaps some nice uniforms in fuchsia and violet . . .

# HARLEQUIN® Temptation

## Secret Fantasies

*Do you have a secret fantasy?*

Kasey Halliday does—she's fallen hard for the "boy" next door. Will Eastman is sexy, sophisticated and definitely interested in Kasey. But there's a mysterious side to this man she can't quite fathom. Find out what Will is hiding in #554 STRANGER IN MY ARMS by Madeline Harper—available in September 1995.

Everybody has a secret fantasy. And you'll find them all in Temptation's exciting new yearlong miniseries, Secret Fantasies. Beginning January 1995, one book each month focuses on the hero's or heroine's innermost romantic desires....

# RUGGED. SEXY. HEROIC.

# OUTLAWS *and* HEROES

Stony Carlton—A lone wolf determined never to be tied down.

Gabriel Taylor—Accused and found guilty by small-town gossip.

Clay Barker—At Revenge Unlimited, he *is* the law.

**JOAN JOHNSTON, DALLAS SCHULZE** and **MALLORY RUSH**, three of romance fiction's biggest names, have created three unforgettable men—modern heroes who have the courage to fight for what is right....

**OUTLAWS AND HEROES**—available in September wherever Harlequin books are sold.

**HARLEQUIN** ®

# MOVE OVER, MELROSE PLACE!

> Apartment for rent
> One bedroom
> Bachelor Arms
> 555-1234

Come live and love in L.A. with the tenants of Bachelor Arms. Enjoy a year's worth of wonderful love stories and meet colorful neighbors you'll bump into again and again.

Startling events from Bachelor Arms' past return to stir up scandal, heartache and painful memories for three of its tenants. Read popular Candace Schuler's three sexy and exciting books to find out how passion, love and betrayal at Bachelor Arms affect the lives of three dynamic men. Bestselling author of over fifteen romance novels, Candace is sure to keep you hooked on Bachelor Arms with her steamy, sensual stories.

**LOVERS AND STRANGERS** #549 (August 1995)

**SEDUCED AND BETRAYED** #553 (September 1995)

**PASSION AND SCANDAL** #557 (October 1995)

Next to move into Bachelor Arms are the heroes and heroines in books by ever-popular Judith Arnold!

**Don't miss the goings-on at Bachelor Arms**

URBAN COWBOYS

# A Stetson and spurs don't make a man a cowboy.

Being a real cowboy means being able to tough it out on the ranch and on the range. Three Manhattan city slickers with something to prove meet that challenge…and succeed.

But are they man enough to handle the three wild western women who lasso their hearts?

Bestselling author Vicki Lewis Thompson will take you on the most exciting trail ride of your life with her fabulous new trilogy— Urban Cowboys.

**THE TRAILBLAZER** #555 (September 1995)

**THE DRIFTER** #559 (October 1995)

**THE LAWMAN** #563 (November 1995)

HARLEQUIN® *Temptation®*

# PRIZE SURPRISE SWEEPSTAKES!

This month's prize:

## BEAUTIFUL WEDGWOOD CHINA!

This month, as a special surprise, we're giving away a bone china dinner service for eight by Wedgwood**, one of England's most prestigious manufacturers!

Think how beautiful your table will look, set with lovely Wedgwood china in the casual Countryware pattern! Each five-piece place setting includes dinner plate, salad plate, soup bowl and cup and saucer.

The facing page contains two Entry Coupons (as does every book you received this shipment). Complete and return *all* the entry coupons; **the more times you enter, the better your chances of winning!**

Then keep your fingers crossed, because you'll find out by September 15, 1995 if you're the winner!

Remember: The more times you enter, the better your chances of winning!*